THE NIGHT HUSTLE

Other Titles by J.F. Moth

Dirby's Express

Dirby's New Home

Dirby's Express 2

Super Weird Magic Book 1

Super Weird Magic Book 2

Super Weird Magic Book 3

Super Weird Magic Book 4

Super Weird Magic Adventures

The Friendly, Unfriendly Witch

Warrior Spirit

The Jewel Thief

Continue the Adventure Part 1

Continue the Adventure Part 2

Blade Quest

The Magical Covered Wagon

Tales of an Ice Horse

The Orb of Time

New Paw City

CONTENTS

CONTENTS

CONTENTS

J.F. MOTH

THE NIGHT HUSTLE

WAREHOUSE - 1 - INT.

WAREHOUSE - 1 - INT.

A blindfold was removed from Milton's eyes and there was silence. Milton knew it wasn't the police; they'd already be asking him questions by now. No, this had to be the mob, the mafia, or some kind of underground organization. The only light that could be seen was that of the moonlight filtering in from the windows high above. Milton could barely see two feet in front of him. Suddenly Milton heard a click and a low hanging lightbulb turn on. His vision slowly came back and he could now see a silhouette of a man appearing against an adjacent wall in this large abandoned ware-house.

Milton's mouth was dry; he felt extremely thirsty. Another body approached him with a large jug of water. He could tell this man was different from the other man who turned on the light bulb purely by his smaller stature and ponytail. The man ripped the duct tape pressed tightly against Milton's mouth.

MILTON

YEEEOOUCCCHH!

The smaller man placed the jug to Milton's lips and poured the water aggressively down his mouth.

Milton struggled to move his hands and legs. He immediately felt the restraints tied around his wrists and ankles as he was tied down to the chair. The water flowed aggressively down Milton's throat. He began to gag. Luckily, the man pulled away the jug. Water regurgitated out of Milton's mouth as he quickly gasped for air. Heavily, Milton breathed in and out, trying to catch his breath.

Milton's head hung low down to his chest. He was finally able to catch his breath, but knew this was only the beginning of some kind of torture experience of some sort.

Milton heard a match strike in the distance and could see the tail of a cigarette being lit.

Another light clicked on, only this time on a small desk with a well dressed man sitting behind it. The man took a long slow drag from his cigarette, kicked his head back, and blew the smoke up towards the ceiling. He wore a tiny monocle tucked tightly into his eye socket and a navy blue suit with a handkerchief tucked neatly inside his suit's chest pocket.

The man behind the desk extinguished his cigarette into a glass ashtray placed near the edge of his desk. He then quickly stood to his feet. Milton could tell this man was the ring-leader of the operation solely by the fear in his cronies' eyes as he walked past them.

He slowly approached Milton, using a wooden cane to support his feeble left leg. When he stood before me, he bent over and looked me straight in the eyes.

MOB BOSS

Mr. Horowitz, where is your friend?

The man sounded like he came from Russian or Eastern European descent. Milton couldn't tell.

MILTON

My friend? I don't know
what you're talking about.
The short man with slicked back hair
straightened his stance.

MOB BOSS

Oh I zink you know
exactly what I'm talking
about.
He began to remove his dark colored leather
glove from his hand.

MOB BOSS

I will ask you one more
time; where is your friend?
As Milton looked up towards the light, he
could see more clearly who this man really
was. It was Yule Upka, a high level Russian
mobster, not even the KGB would dare to mess
with.

MILTON

I told you, I don't know
what you're talking about.
Upka raised his bare hand and quickly
smacked Milton across the face.
WHACK!

MILTON

Ouch!

UPKA

Fine, then. If you won't answer me, then maybe you'll answer my associate.

The small Russian mobster snapped his finger.

UPKA

Boris, removed his nuts!

MILTON

What! My nuts? Nooo!

A third man appeared from the shadows with a chainsaw. He quickly revved its engine and started the hedge cutting machine, which was about to become the end of Milton's manhood as he knew it.

MILTON

AHHH!!

(The camera freezes on Milton's face.)

Truth of the matter is Milton actually had no idea where his friend was. His friend's name was Ramijan. A typical smart, scruffy haired, skinny Indian guy. Milton knew he was into bit-coin trading, but had no idea he'd be dealing with dangerous men like this.

But no way in a million years would Milton have even predicted he'd end up in a situation like this! He, after all, was just a local food delivery guy. Yup, that's right. Milton worked for Food Hub, you know, one of those side hustle, app gigs, everyone jumped on during the pandemic. It's actually kind of a long story, so let me just go back and tell you from the beginning...

His name was Milton, Milton Horowitz, and about a year ago, he was your ordinary, single guy living on Long Island, New York. He lived in a town called Laurel Valley. It's about twenty five minutes away from one of the greatest cities on the planet; New York City that is. Funny I should say planet. Milton was actually teaching English as a Second Language to students from all around the world. Online of course, through a company called Global-E. He taught out of his apartment, which is connected to a nice house in a very safe wholesome suburban neighborhood.

WANG APARTMENT - INT.

WANG APARTMENT - INT.

(Scene with Milton conducting a lesson with a Chilean student.)

On this very day, Milton's life started to spin upside down. He was tutoring one of his favorite students named Giorgio who was from Chile and very friendly.

Gorgio was discussing his family life and what he was going to do for the upcoming weekend.

GIORGIO

And then you will take my wife and you will take her out to dinner. You will then take my wife to a movie, and if you are lucky, you will kiss my wife. Then, you will take my wife home and sleep with my wife and make sweet sweet love to my wife.

Now a good teacher would have corrected him, but Milton, he simply didn't have the heart to tell Giorgio that he meant his wife. So...

MILTON

Excellent, Giorgio! I'm sure the two of us will have a great time together!

Giorgio smiled with confusion.

MILTON

Alright, Giorgio! Great lesson today and I'll see you next time!

Gorgio's expression of confusion quickly changed to a friendly smile and waved good-bye.

CHAPTER

3

WANG APARTMENT - EXT.

WANG APARTMENT - EXT.

Yup, it was just another ordinary day for Milton; teach his students during the day, hang-out with his friends and play a little pickleball at dusk, and then drive for Food-Hub at night. So that was the plan at least. Milton remembered leaving the house that day feeling pretty good about life. No complaints really. He lived in a nice apartment, which was attached to his landlord's house. They were a friendly Chinese-American couple and such sweet people. On his way out of the driveway, he noticed Mrs. Wang working on her garden. By accident he ran over her raspberry plants.

MILTON

Sorry Mrs. Wang!

Milton apologized, sticking his head a quarter of the way out of the window. The sweet older lady smiled and waved her hand as Milton continued to back out of the driveway.

MRS. WANG

That stupid jerk!

Kindly, she continued to wave as Milton drove away with his 2016 Nissan Sentra.

ROAD SCENE - 1 - EXT.

ROAD SCENE - 1 - EXT.

(Driving through the town.)

Yes, Laurel Valley, Long Island was a quaint little town, filled with the happiest and kindest people around. Milton pulled up to a traffic light and looked to his right. He noticed a minivan with a lady talking on her mobile device and her child looking directly at him through the closed window. She looked like a kind innocent little girl, so Milton politely smiled and waved at her. Her cute little stare, however, suddenly turned into a mean, weathered scowl, to which she then placed the back of her fist against the window and flipped Milton the bird.

Milton was thrown back. His eyes blossomed wide. The light turned green and away they drove with her cute middle finger pinned against the window and her scowl that quickly turned into a devious and twisted little smile.

That's when things started to feel weird for Milton. But he didn't think much of it. He still had the whole night ahead of him. And a fun match of pickleball with his friends to look forward to.

CHAPTER

5

PICKLEBALL PARK - EXT.

PICKLEBALL PARK - EXT.

When Milton pulled into the parking lot of the pickleball courts, he could see his two friends waiting there for him. Their names were Josh Benson and Fritz Parker. Benson wore thick, dark rimmed glass and sported a crew cut. Parker was your typical free spirit with a man bun and scruffy beard.

Milton grew up with these guys here in Laurel Valley. They all graduated from Laurel Valley High School together, but split ways after college. Apparently they didn't go too far away though as the three found each other again after college. Benson was a film graduate from Long Island University. He worked for a media company filming mostly Bar mitzvahs and weddings. Parker was an art minor at our local community college. He's actually pretty good; known around these parts for his mural work, a.k.a graffiti tagging. But a lot of it is actually pretty impressive. At least we think so. The local police department definitely thinks otherwise. Most of the time, we could find him working at a local picture frame shop near his uncle's delicatessen.

I shut off my car playing hard death-metal and approached my friends sitting on the courts. Benson was smoking a cigarette and Parker was looking up Asian porn websites on his cell phone.

MILTON

Where's Ramijan?

Benson and Parker unenthusiastically shrugged their shoulders.

MILTON

Uh, I think we need four
people to play doubles.

PARKER

Oh, here he is now.

Parker's ringtone blasted, '*Oh My God, Me so horny!*' over and over In a thick Asian accent.

PARKER

He says he's too sick to
play today. He also says go
ahead and play without me
butt-heads!

Ramijan really had a way with words. He ironically received a perfect score on his SAT's back in high school and was accepted into Harvard. He studied English for two semesters and dropped out. These days, he's been working on a bit-coin currency platform. None of them really know what he's doing half of the time.

MILTON

Great! Just Great So how
are we going to play dou-
bles? I hate playing pickleball singles. There's so
much bending over to pick
up this damn plastic ball!

Perchance, a voice could be heard coming from the other side of the pickleball courts.

MR. BARLEY

Hey, you young panty-snappers! Looks like you can use another pickleball player to even out the sides!

It was old Mr. Barley. He had impeccable timing for whenever Ramijan couldn't show. The three of us lowered our heads in disappointment. Don't get me wrong, Mr. Barley was a nice guy, but sometimes he could seem a little... much.

MR. BARLEY

I bought my new paddles from Dickmart! Figured I'd give them a spin!

MILTON

Oh, hey Mr. Barely.

Milton looked at Benson and Parker, waiting for them to chime in, but there was dead silence.

MILTON

Uh, yeah. I guess you can fill in for Ramijan.

MR. BARLEY

Oh, that's fantastic! Let me just settle myself here in the corner and stretch out my nads!

The old man placed his right foot upon the court's bench and lunged himself forward in an awkward stretch. Thankfully, it was getting colder outside and the summer heat was coming to an end. Otherwise, we would literally have seen his old nads stretching.

MR. BARLEY

Alright you sissy gophers! Let's see what you got!

MILTON

OK, Benson, you play on Mr. Barley's team. Parker, you stay here with me on this side. We'll serve first.

Everyone took their positions.

MR. BARLEY

Alright, sonny! Let's see what you got!

Milton served it into play and hit it to Benson. Benson returned the shot and hit the ball with a good amount of speed towards Parker. Parker was slow to react and popped the ball high into the air, setting it up perfectly for old Mr. Barley to spike it down; which is exactly what he did.

MR. BARLEY

HA! You can't beat the old Barleymeister!

The old man raised his hand for a high five towards Benson.

Benson, nonchalantly ignored his older teammate and walked back to his side. Mr. Barely high fived the air and returned to his return position as well. Milton threw the ball back to Mr. Barely who caught it and prepared himself to serve.

MR. BARLEY

Alright there, pillow-fluffer! 1-0-1!" Mr. Barely called.

Parker and Milton prepared themselves. The ball was now being served to Parker.

MILTON

OK, Parker, you got this!

WACK!

Mr. Barley served it to Parker, however, Parker hit the ball directly into the net. Milton could have called that one, knowing Parker was the weakest player on the court.

MR. BARLEY
Ha! Can't handle my serving their sonny!

MILTON
It's alright Parker. Keep your head up. You'll get this next one.

Parker nodded his head and caught his breath. Milton tossed the ball back to Mr. Barley who again called the score.

MR. BARLEY
2-0-2!

Mr. Barely suddenly paused and looked into the sky. He scratched his chin.

MR. BARLEY
You know, there Mr. Parker, I remember your dad when he was younger and you remind me of him. He too was a light loading wingle worm like yourself! Back

in Nam we'd have called both of
you feather-foot sissies and made
you fluff platoon's pillows for us!
Ha!

Milton looked at Parker and could see the rage growing inside his eyes. Old man Barley, however, continued to laugh out loud in an extremely rude way.

MILTON

Alright, Mr. Barley. Can we
bring the bantering to a mini-
mum. I have to work after this
and we don't have all night.

Mr. Barley's laughter broke into a coughing fit. Benson pulled his head back with one brow raised, trying not to catch the old man's germs.

What happened next was extremely unlucky for old Mr. Barley. It was as if it all went down in slow motion. The old man dropped the ball and let it bounce on the hard cement court. The ball bounced back up to his knees, where he served the ball once again into Parker's direction. The ball cleared the kitchen line and bounced into play. Milton glanced to his left and noticed Parker's face was still enraged with anger.

With all his might, Parker wound the pickleball racket behind his body and crushed the ball with an incredible amount of force. They were all stunned. They didn't know Parker had it in him. The ball soared back over the net and flew directly into the old man's direction. Mr. Barley was too slow to move out of the way and unfortunately for him, the ball nailed him squarely in the forehead.

BOOSH!

The old man's eyes shut tight and down he went, hard on his back. Milton stepped forward with concern. Benson ran to his fallen partner and looked at him with a grimace.

BENSON

Dude, I think you killed Mr. Barley!

Both Parker and Milton ran to the old man remaining knocked out on the ground. The three of them were now all hovering over Mr. Barley, waiting for him to wake up.

BENSON

Parker, what did you do?

PARKER

I don't know! I blanked out!

BENSON

What do you mean, you blanked out! You just nailed Mr. Barley in the head with a pickleball!

Parker simply shrugged his shoulders not knowing how to reply. Suddenly, the old man's leg began to twitch.

PARKER

Look, he's not dead. He's still moving!

BENSON

You know, I heard somewhere that the deceased can still move around a bit when they first die. I think it's called rigamortis or something.

PARKER

Thanks for the tidbit, jackass!

Thankfully, however, Mr. Barley began to moan.

MILTON

Look, he's waking up! C'mon, let's help him out!

Carefully, the three of us sat him up.

MILTON
Mr. Barley, are you alright?

MR. BARLEY
Who, me? What happened?

Mr. Barley rubbed his head.

PARKER
We thought you died!

MILTON
Parker! Shhh!

Milton nudged Parker's arm with his elbow.

MR. BARLEY
It's gonna take a whole lot more to kill old Bruce Barley! You know I once fought an entire fleet of tanks in Nam by myself!

MILTON
Alright, alright, Mr. Barely. Let's get you onto that bench over there.

The three of them lifted Mr. Barely and walked him to the side of the court where a metal bench was located.

BENSON

Great, there goes our pickleball game for the day.

MILTON

It's alright, I should start to dash. You two play each other in a singles match. I'll catch up with ya later.

PARKER

Dude, why are you still dashing? You can easily just go work for my uncle, Frank, at the deli.

MILTON

Nah, I'm good. I can't do early mornings. I'm more of an evening shift guy. Plus, I like the independence of the job. I can work whenever I want and don't have a boss breathing down my neck. It also gives me time to write my best selling novel.

PARKER

Yea, right. You've been writing that thing for the past three years now.

MILTON

Hey, greatness takes time, my man.

Parker rolled his eyes.

BENSON

Or you could work with me and Baxter shooting weddings and Batmitzfahs. There's some serious milf action at these events.

MILTON

Uh, er, I'll think about it. Thanks for the offer.

BENSON

Alright, suit yourself. But, F.Y.I. You two are both missin' out on some primo over 50 game!

MILTON

Right... Thanks Benson, I'll keep that in mind.

Milton lifted his wrist and looked at his watch.

MILTON

OK gents, time for the diner crowd. I'll shoot you both a text later on and see where you're all at. Maybe we can meet up at Rami-jan's house and play some online Battle-Warfare or something.

PARKER

That's if he isn't too busy with his crypto-bit-shoot.

MILTON

True. Alright, I'm gonna bounce. Catch ya later.

MR. BARLEY

Hey! Where you goin!

MILTON

I gotta run to work, Mr. Barely. Glad to see you're still alive.

MR. BARLEY

There ain't nothin' that can destroy Bruce the bull!

Old man Barely quickly stood to his feet, but immediately began to feel dizzy. Luckily, Parker and Benson were there to catch him before he fell again. Milton waved goodbye and headed back to his car. Milton threw his pickleball paddle inside his trunk and found himself back inside the driver's seat, ready to begin his night. Milton turned on the app and at last, his night was about to begin. This was where things were about to get weirder and weirder as the night went on.

PARKING LOT - NEAR JORGE'S SOUTHWEST BURRITO BAR - EXT.

PARKING LOT - NEAR JORGE'S SOUTHWEST BUR-RITO BAR - EXT.

Milton switched his headlights on as the sun already began to set. He grabbed the mini controller to his seat's heating pad and plugged the pad into his car's cigarette lighter. He banged on the controller, which didn't seem to work.

Milton

Damn thing never works! Ahh just forget it!

Milton tossed the controller over his shoulder, which landed on the seats behind him. The pad however remained plugged in. Its wires looked frayed and the cigarette lighter appeared to be broken; something Milton put on his list of things to fix later on.

He found himself on a busy main street when his first trip gave him an alert. Milton accepted the trip, which had him go to Jorge's Southwest Burrito Bar.

Everything went as planned when he picked up the food. No complaints and all friendly smiles from the Latin-American employees at the restaurant. Milton hopped back into his car with the food and confirmed his pick up on the app.

Though, while leaving the parking lot, Milton did run into a weird altercation of some sort. You see, he was behind a large SUV that was stopped at a stop sign. Milton noticed his rear view tail-light glowing bright red as the large man oddly began to back up. Milton was caught off guard and delayed to back up as well. When Milton finally realized what was happening, he too began to place his car in reverse. But by that point, the driver of the large SUV ran out of patience and exited his car. As Milton was now slowly backing up, the large man found his way to Milton's window and knocked his stocky knuckle against it.

LARGE MAN

Hey, jackass! Can't you see, I'm
trying to back up here!

Milton's eyes grew wide, surprised he would come out to inform him of what Milton already knew. Milton was a bit slow in addressing the situation, it's true, but to be fair, Milton did back up for the pro-wrestler look-alike who now towered over his 2016 Nissan Sentra. Something, however, raged inside of Milton. He neglected the fact that the large man could rip him out of the car without breaking a sweat. Milton was mad. He was known for losing his patience on the streets from time to time. It's road rage. Sure we should all refrain from bursting out, but hey, sometimes it just happens.

LARGE MAN

Can't you see! I'm trying to
park into that spot!

Luckily, the large man started to back away from Milton, yet gave him a watch-it-bud look as he slowly walked back to his car.

MILTON

I was backing up for you and I
think it's fair to say that from my

point of view, I couldn't see exactly what you were trying to do!

The big man paused in front of Milton's car. At this point Milton thought, *Oh shoot. This guy's going to hulk smash the hood of my car!*

Milton braced himself and slowly rolled up the window.

LARGE MAN

You're crazy, man!

Again, Milton's anger and frustration got the best of him.

MILTON

I'm crazy, you're the guy who came up to my window! And another thing, what the hell were you going to do?

The giant of a man faced Milton.

Again, Milton thought, *yup he's definitely going to act out a street-fighter-bonus-stage scene and destroy my car right now.*

Though, what he did next was even stranger. The large man simply tilted his head back and belted a most menacing laugh that shook Milton's entire car.

At this point for sure Milton knew he was a goner. The large man quickly placed his huge gorilla-like hands on Milton's car-hood and instantly stopped laughing.

Oh shoot, oh shoot, oh shoot, Milton thought. *Milton, your big mouth has finally got you in over your head on this one.*

Yet, to Milton's luck, an innocent old lady walking up to their little confrontation.

LITTLE OLD LADY

Hey, you! Big guy! Get back in
your car!

The man's scowl quickly turned into a friendly smile.

LARGE MAN

Sorry ma'am, everything's fine
here. I'm just having a little chat
with my new friend here.

LITTLE OLD LADY

I said, get back in your car!

The large beast of a man looked at Milton one last time with anger, but gave into the old lady's request. Ultimately he hopped inside his car and drove away.

Milton lowered his window.

MILTON

Geez thanks, lady. You just saved my life... and my car!

LITTLE OLD LADY

No sweat, young man. Next time you should learn to keep your cool around larger, angrier, people like that.

MILTON

Yes, ma'am.

LITTLE OLD LADY

Alright, then, enjoy the rest of your night.

MILTON

Yea, you, you too!

Milton slowly drove away. But as he looked back at his phone, Milton noticed he was now running late for his Food Dash order.

MILTON

Oh crap! I'm going to be late!

ROAD SCENE 2 - DESTINATION 1 - EXT.

ROAD SCENE 2 - DESTINATION 1 - EXT.

Milton floored the gas pedal and peeled out of the parking lot. The Food Dash application rates its dashers on their service. There's a whole point system monitoring tardiness, friendliness, and the overall completion of the tasks. The more points you receive, the higher your rating is. With a higher rating, you are able to dash whenever you wish; that is not only when the area is busy with hungry customers. This is why a Food Dasher would want to drop off his deliveries in a timely fashion of course other than to keep customers from waiting.

So there Milton was, coasting down a Long Island main street. There were other cars out on the road, but it wasn't anything like the Long Island traffic we are all used to during rush hour. Though, there were some Sunday drivers out at night. Usually it was young guys in their Dodge Chargers or modified racing cars. That or old, rich men taking their $80,000 BMWs out for a spin at night.

Oddly enough, as it was turning out to be this kind of a night for the young dasher, Milton did run into a minivan whose driver thought he was Jeff Gordon racing in NASCAR's Brickyard 400. Milton also was going pretty fast, but of course, he was being mindful of the speed limit at least.

Milton looked back in his rearview mirror and could see the white minivan closing in on his right-hand side. He tried to speed up as the minivan came closer and closer, but Jeff Gordan of minivans was coming in way too hot.

VRRROOOMMM!

The minivan whizzed straight past Milton in the right lane. Now, Milton normally would let these drag racers, or in this case, this speed racin' soccer mom, pass by. But, Milton was in rare form. He was compelled to slow this lady down and remind her of the speed limit. Thus, again, Milton floored the pedal to the metal and sped up to the Mario Andretti driving-housewife.

The minivan was now directly in front of Milton. It then placed its right directional blinker on and moved back into the right lane, giving Milton an opportune time to speed up and drive neck and neck with the roadster. And that's exactly what Milton did. He was now adjacent to the minivan. To Milton's surprise, when he looked to his right, he noticed that she was a he! It was a man with his wife sitting in the passenger seat and his children riding in the back seat.

Family or not, Milton was going to teach this man a lesson. But, what was Milton going to do with this minivan family? He asked himself the same question. To be honest Milton had no idea. The only thing he could think of was to give the minivan man an unfriendly death-stare.

So there they were, neck and neck. Milton was looking at him, and he looked back at Milton. Of course they had to keep their eyes on the road as well, but we were in a driver-to-driver staring contest and it was him against Milton.

Now, of course, this battle couldn't go on forever. They were soon to hit a traffic light eventually. Thus, when they reached the oncoming red light, they continued to stare at each other. All Milton could think of - was to beat him in the staring competition. Polite?

Neighborly? Maybe not. A bit disturbing? Maybe yes. But Milton was pissed. It was just that kind of day.

So there they were at the stop light. The stare off ensued. The minivan man lowered his window as did Milton. He then whipped out his fist and flipped Milton the bird.

MINIVAN MAN

Do you not have a brain?

MINIVAN MAN'S WIFE

No! Stop, honey! He might be
a terrorist!

Milton continued to stare as the minivan man continued to wave his middle finger.

The minivan man then whipped out his other hand and gave Milton another middle finger.

MINIVAN MAN

Here you go buddy! Look, I have two for you!

So as Milton continued to stare with rage, the man laughed at him, waving his two middle fingers with pride.

MINIVAN MAN'S WIFE

No, honey stop that! Don't do this here!
There are policemen right over there!

She was right. There were two parked policemen in the street perpendicular to where we were stopped for the light. Milton was Ok with that though. The minivan man looked bigger than him, and if shoot was about to go down, then at least Milton could call for help. Milton held his ground, though, and continued to stare. But in the end, the light turned green.

Milton drove forward and the double-fisting-bird-flipper-family guy turned right. He went his way and Milton went his, never to see each other ever again.

Milton was proud of himself for not backing down, but knew he'd feel like an idiot for even messing with a crazy driver like that. Milton didn't have time to mull over the idea. He looked at his app which alerted him in bold red letters:

You have exactly one minute before this trip is considered late!

MILTON

Oh crap!

Milton switched the Food Dash app back to his GPS app and noticed he was now two minutes away. Milton knew however, that he could still make it to the drop off point on time though. Quickly, the young dasher turned into the local neighborhood where he zig-zagged up and down its winding hills. Milton switched the GPS app back to the Food Dash app and noticed he had twenty seconds remaining. There were two stop signs to go and after that was his final destination. Milton approached the first stop sign and made a legitimate stop. He then floored it to the next stop sign and again stopped on a dime, causing himself to hurl forward in his seat. Milton's head was now extremely close to his mounted mobile phone on the dashboard vent. The Food Dash app began its ten second countdown.

Milton knew he could still make it as he was only four houses away. Milton immediately pushed the pedal down and gave the engine gas, hurling him back into his seat. The countdown continued, 7,6,5...

HOUSE - 1 - DOOR STEP - EXT.

HOUSE - 1 - DOOR STEP - EXT.

At last, Milton made it to the driveway and came to a screeching halt, causing his body to fly back into his steering wheel. In one motion, however, Milton dismounted his phone, held the food in front of the camera's lens and took a pseudo-selfie with the customer's house in the background. And with one second left, Milton completed the task. Yeah, technically the dashers are supposed to take a picture of the food left on the doorstep, but in this case, Milton was just happy to make it there on time with all the odd mishaps that happened along the way.

Happily, Milton opened the door and hopped out of his car. He approached the door and placed the bag of Mexican cuisine on the house's outside door mat. Though, before Milton could leave the front porch, the customer walked outside and quickly picked up the delivery.

MILTON

Have a good night!

The customer remained quiet. Milton paused in his tracks, sensing the customer was dissatisfied with something.

MILTON

Is everything OK, sir?

The man was large. Not as big as the giant in the parking lot a few moments ago, but he was wide and burly. The man was full of tattoos on his body and wore a tightly-fitted, white wife-beater. He lifted the delivery high to his face and noticed a water bottle resting at the bottom of the bag, which caused him to raise a brow.

HANGRY MAN

This isn't my food.

MILTON

Are you Anthony?

HANGRY MAN

Yes, but this isn't my order.

MILTON

Uh, it should be sir, it has your
name on the bag.

Milton took a step toward him to help him out.
The customer inspected the delivery again and continued to focus on the water bottle seen through the
clear plastic bag.

HANGRY MAN

I didn't order a water bottle.
This isn't my order.

Now, Milton had a feeling that somehow the restaurant was giving away free water bottles due to the
recent COVID outbreak about eight months ago, but
he wasn't quite sure.

MILTON

Uh, maybe you can give them
a call and tell them they messed
up the order. Most likely they

will send you another order. Free
food, right?

The guy wasn't having it. He wanted his order and
he wanted his order now. He was hangry. And let me
tell you from experience, hangry people are crazy! By
the way, the word hangry is when someone is both
hungry and angry. It's a very volatile combination.

HANGRY MAN
I want you to call them, you're
the Food Dasher.

Now Milton's gut instinct was to just get out of
there. He needed to continue with the night and
make his quota. And truthfully, this was an issue
between the customer and the restaurant. OK, OK,
Milton could have helped the hangry man and called
for support, but that would have taken another
twenty minutes or so. And afterall, Milton's just the
middleman. What's the old saying? Don't shoot the
messenger, right?

Milton quickly remembered that he left his phone
in the car.

MILTON
OK, sir, give me one minute, I
just got to get my phone. I'll be
right back.

HANGRY MAN

Alright, but don't you go dri-
vin' off on me!

MILTON

Sure, sure!

Milton lied. His plan was to hop in the car and get the hell out of dodge. OK OK, I know this doesn't sound ethical, but c'mon, Milton made all of $5.50. Plus the hangry man had the right order and could have easily called Food Dasher himself if for some reason the order wasn't correct. In the long run, the customer would have been sent another order and been eating like a king.

CHAPTER

9

ROAD SCENE - 3 - HANGRY MAN CHASE - EXT.

ROAD SCENE - 3 - HANGRY MAN CHASE - EXT.

So there Milton was back in the car. He looked in his rearview mirror and noticed the hangry man was still fixated on the free water bottle squashed at the bottom of the bag. Thus, with the customer not looking, Milton instantly turned the engine on and peeled away from the curb. Milton looked back in the rearview mirror once more and could see the hangry man running after him. The hangry man was screaming obscenities and was completely livid. OK OK, you might be thinking, Milton, that was terrible customer service. But hey, when you're delivering orders at night and something doesn't feel right, Milton always says it's best to just get the hell out of there.

Thus, as Milton drove further and further away, the burly, hangry man became smaller and smaller. At last, Milton completed the trip with his mind set on the next.

For the next minute or so, life appeared to be alright. Milton put on some tunes, sang along to a classic rock song and continued with his dash.

Though, after Milton turned back onto the main street, he could see the singular headlight of a Harley Davidson motorcycle coming up behind him in his side view mirror. Milton refocused on the road and continued to hum carelessly to the classic rock song playing on the radio. Milton's gut instincts caused him to become worrisome. Yes, something about this oncoming motorcycle started to concern him.

Milton looked back in the rearview mirror and there he was! It was the burly, hangry man! With goggles over his eyes and an old style helmet, his angry face became clearer and clearer. It was indeed him.

MILTON

Oh shoot!

So there Milton was, in another pickle, now being chased by a member of hell's angels! Milton sped up, hoping to lose the mad biker, but his Nissan Sentra was no match for this guy's Harley modeled crotch-rocket.

He immediately swerved around Milton's tail and approached the young dasher from the side. Milton looked to his left and could see the hangry man yelling at him like a madman. Thankfully, Milton's window was up and all he could see was the hangry man's lips smacking and his finger pointing directly at him.

For the second time this evening, Milton surely thought he was going to get murdered.

Milton kept his car steady and tried to somehow figure a way out of this mess. Though, to his misfortune, a traffic light was approaching, as this was Long Island and not the German autobahn.

MILTON

Damnit!

Milton had no choice, he had to stop at the light, regardless if he was going to get himself killed or not.

They both slowed down and met each other at the light. The hangry man continued to yell, but all Milton could see was his gums flapping all over the place.

Milton bravely opened the window and could now hear his scream.

HANGRY MAN

Did you steal my food?

MILTON

No, sir. The food I gave you is yours! They must have given you a free, complimentary water bottle.

The hangry biker looked at me with fury in his eyes.

HANGRY MAN

Did you steal my food!

MILTON

NO, SIR! I didn't steal your food! Go back and see for yourself. Your order should be in that bag. If it isn't your order, just call the restaurant so they can refund you your money! Plus, you can keep whatever food is in that bag! Hey, free food!

The man continued to give Milton a death stare, though at this point he finally ran out of things to yell.

The light finally turned green. Milton took that as an opportunity to end the conversation and quickly escape. He immediately hit the gas pedal and, again, peeled away from the hangry customer. Milton looked in my rearview mirror and could see him following me.

MILTON

What is it with this guy!

Finally, Milton could see him falling further and further behind as the hangry man ultimately turned back into his neighborhood development.

Geez, what a crazy start to a night! Well, it can only get better from here, so Milton thought.

ROAD SCENE 4 - PICK UP 2 - EXT.

Milton's heart beat finally began to settle. He slowly caught his breath and continued with his dash. He reopened his dash app, but wasn't receiving any alerts for trips, so Milton continued to drive back into a busier part of the district in which he worked.

Perchance, Milton's phone rang. It was Ramijan.

MILTON

Yo, Ramijan, what's up my man?

RAMIJAN

Yo, yo, yo, what up playa!
Where you been?

MILTON

Ah, just workin' Rami. What you been up to? Still makin' bank with that crypto-nonsense?

RAMIJAN

You know it, son! I just sold 200 Ethereum to a whack group of Russian investors.

MILTON

Wow, is that good?

RAMIJAN

Hell yea, playa! I bought that early crypto shizat when it was fresh off the grill, son. Gonna buy me a nice house for myself.

MILTON

Sounds nice.

RAMIJAN

Once I move out of my mom's basement that is.

MILTON

I feel ya.

Milton's app suddenly gave him an alert for another trip.

MILTON

Yo, Rami, I gotta bounce, I'm driving the dash now.

RAMIJAN

Alright, son. Do your thang!

MILTON

Thanks, Rami.

RAMIJAN

Hey, you comin' over later with the boys for some Battle Warfare?

MILTON

Maybe, I'll see how much loot I've made. Kinda havin' a slow start, so we'll see.

RAMIJAN

Alright, playa! Keep in touch.

MILTON

Alright, sounds good, sounds good. I'll talk to you later.

RAMIJAN

Aight, peace out, homeboy!

MILTON

Aight, later, Rami.

The call ended, the Food Dash app reappeared on Milton's phone. He scrolled down to see what restaurant would be next, and low and behold, it was their local fast food chain named Chattanooga's Home-fries. It was your everyday burger-taco-hotdog-fries-milkshake joint. There were only two on the island, this being the original location right here in Milton's very own home-town of Laurel Valley. The other was located across the harbor in Port Wallington.

The night started a bit rocky for Milton. But all was good now. And let me tell you, there have been some interesting dashes in the past for the young dasher.

FLASHBACK SCENE - DOORSTEP - EXT.

FLASHBACK SCENE - DOORSTEP - EXT.

One time, Milton had an open container of creamer from Donut Palace in his trunk with a big order of doughnuts. Well, when he stopped short due to an old lady cutting him off at a traffic light, the creamer spilt all over his trunk's carpet. The smell of rancid milk lingered inside Milton's car for the entire summer. It was awful.

There was another time where Milton made the delivery with no problem. He dropped off the package at the door and happily completed the task. But, on his way back to the car, an innocent older lady approached him.

Now Milton thought she was the owner of the home.

MILTON

Your package is by the front door ma'am.

GROOVER LADY

I don't live here. I actually work for Groover Eats.

She paused to grab a brown paper bag.

GROOVER LADY

Oh, young man, would you mind placing this package at the front door. My back is killing me!

MILTON

Uh, yea sure no problem.

Milton dropped the food at the door feeling a little bit perturbed, but then thought, *hey, why not help a fellow delivery-person out right?*

On his way back, the PSU Delivery man pulled his large blue van up to Milton's car. Milton acknowledged the delivery man with a wave.

The delivery man then reached his arm out of his open side door.

PSU MAN
Hey, brother-man, do you mind carrying this box to the front door. My back is killing me.

Now getting a bit angry, I presented the delivery guy with a fake smile and agreed to help him out.

PSU MAN
Thanks, brother-man!

After dropping that package on the front door stoop, Milton looked around to see if any other delivery van or car was coming. To his surprise, the Ex-Fed delivery truck came flying down the street.

MILTON
You gotta be kidding me!

Milton hurriedly walked back to his car and peeled out, wishing not to help any other drivers, knowing if he did, then his back would surely be bothering him, as if it didn't already!

Now it's worth mentioning that Food Dashing was not all that bad. There were little perks while working with Food Dash here and there. One benefit was being part of a company which provided their local communities with a convenient food delivering service. The other perk, for Milton at least, was going to Chattanooga's where he could see one of his favorite fast food workers. He didn't know her name, but man he had the hots for her! Milton thought this girl was beautiful; a super ten-out-of-ten beauty. Milton just wished he had the right words to say to her whenever he would see her. It's like his brain would go numb and he wouldn't be able to think straight for some reason.

Anyways, it was Friday. She always worked on Friday nights. Thus, happily, Milton drove to the restaurant, feeling good about life and listening to his favorite tunes in his car.

CHATTANOOGA'S DRIVE-THRU 1 - EXT.

CHATTANOOGA'S DRIVE-THRU 1 - EXT.

When Milton reached his destination, he drove up to the drive thru line.

WELCOME TO CHATTANOOGA'S

There was only one car ahead of him, which gave Milton enough time to settle in and confirm his arrival on the app. He noticed the name for this trip was Fuda. F.U.D.A.

Milton pulled up to the drive thru speaker and was greeted by a male cashier.

CHATTANOOGA EMPLOYEE

Hi, welcome to Chattanooga's, may I take your order?

MILTON

Yea, um pick up for Food Dash.

CHATTANOOGA EMPLOYEE

OK, Food Dash. What's the name?" the worker asked.

MILTON

Fuda.

CHATTANOOGA EMPLOYEE

What's the name?

MILTON

Fuda.

CHATTANOOGA EMPLOYEE

What's the name?

MILTON

Fuda?

CHATTANOOGA EMPLOYEE
What's the name?

MILTON
Fuda! The name's Fuda!

CHATTANOOGA EMPLOYEE
OK...

There was a moment of silence.

MILTON
What's the name?

Milton started to lose his patience, but quickly reminded himself to keep it together.

MILTON
The name's Fuda! F.U.D.A! Fuda
is the name. I'm making a pick-
up with Food Dash!

Another moment of silence ensued.
Milton squinted into the bright lights of the out-door menu blaring him directly in the face.

CHATTANOOGA EMPLOYEE
OK, drive around to the second window.

Oh my God, finally, Milton thought to himself.

When he pulled around, Milton now found himself parked behind five other cars.

MILTON

Damnit!

Milton fixed his seating position, trying to get comfortable in his driver's seat. He knew he'd be waiting for a while. When Milton finally found a somewhat comfortable position, he looked up into the sky and noticed it was now fully dark outside. The moon hung high in the star-filled sky and lit the empty parking lot that was located to his right.

Milton's phone buzzed unexpectedly. He pulled the phone off his vent-mount and noticed it was a text from Parker. It read:

PARKER'S TEXT

Hey, jerk-face! We just got to Rami's. Gonna play some Battle Warfare. You comin'?

Milton noticed the line hadn't moved and knew he'd be on this queue for at least another 20 minutes.

Milton replied:

MILTON'S TEXT

I don't know man. Havin' a slow start. I'll try to make it later. Probably be super late.

Parker replied:

PARKER'S TEXT
Alright, later jerk-face!

Milton swiped away the message and looked up to see if the line had moved at all. It didn't move an inch. Milton turned the engine off, placed his right foot on the dashboard, and nestled in his seat to play a bit of online chess.

To Milton's surprise, he was rudely disturbed by a car honk

HIGH SCHOOL GUY
Yo! Wake the damnit up!

It startled Milton. He looked up and realized the line had finally moved. Milton quickly turned on my ignition and pulled ahead. He was happy the line was finally moving, but now slightly agitated that there was a group of young high school kids acting up behind him. Milton was at that age about ten years ago, he understood, but these kids were obnoxious to say the least. They were blasting techno house music, which Milton had nothing against, but its bass was vibrating their car's entire frame. Plus, they were running in and out of the car, chasing each other in the parking lot and causing such a scene. But hey, Milton got it, they were young, so he just minded his own business. It just added a bit of chaos to the line, that's all.

So there Milton was with only two more cars ahead of him. Milton continued to play chess on his phone, but could still hear the teenagers running wild behind him. Especially when they ordered.

During their order, Milton heard a young girl's voice.

HIGH SCHOOL GIRL

Yeah, I want a six piece chicken
nugget combo and an iced water!

HIGH SCHOOL GUY

Why are you getting water? It's not gonna make your meal any healthier. You're just gonna smoke afterwards anyways!

HIGH SCHOOL GIRL

Donny, I thought I told you to shut up damnit!

CHATTANOOGA EMPLOYEE

Can I get you anything else?"
the Chattanooga employee asked.

HIGH SCHOOL GIRL

No, that's it. Did you get my large iced water? Don't forget about my large iced water.

CHATTANOOGA EMPLOYEE

Yes, ma'am. That'll be $8.37. Please drive to the second window.

The girl's obnoxious voice finally came to a lull, but the loud techno music quickly returned, including its loud vibrating bass.

17 minutes later, when Milton finally made it to the drive-thru window, he was greeted with the bright lights of Chattanooga's interior kitchen and drive-thru register counter. It was filled with Latin-American workers. Maybe more than the employees at Jorge's Southwest Burrito Bar. It surely was a sign of the times with American fast food employment.

A nice young man with a dark mustache approached the window.

VICTOR

Name?

Immediately, Milton recognized who he was. It was Victor, the restaurant's kind Peruvian employee. Milton has known Victor for the past three years now. Yes, Victor has done quite well for himself here at Chattanooga's, climbing all the way to night shift manager.

MILTON

Fuda, por favor.

He looked up and quickly noticed who I was by my poor attempt at Spanish.

VICTOR

Caballero! ¡Cómo estás, mi amigo!

MILTON

Muy bien, ¿y tú?

VICTOR

¡Bien gracias, Caballero! Nombre?

MILTON

Fuda, por favor!

Milton always felt cool replying in Spanish, even if he knew a little less than a toddler.

VICTOR

Un momento amigo. Let me go check on the order" he responded.

When Victor stepped away from the register to retrieve the order, the beautiful young female

Chattanooga employee, that Milton adored so much, could finally be seen.

Ahh, there she was. It was love at first sight every time Milton saw her. And she had an amazing Latin booty that could even put J-lo's ass to shame. Milton stared at her with stars in his eyes as he filled the little plastic cups with Chattanooga fries. She looked up and made eye contact with Milton. Milton panicked as he always did and quickly looked away, trying to not appear too much like a crazy stalker.

This time, however, Milton mustered up the courage and looked back at her. The two of them locked eyes. It was an incredible feeling to say the least.

But like a record scratching during a beautiful Vivaldi symphony, the obnoxious girl behind me yelled something.

HIGH SCHOOL GIRL
Stop scratchin' your ass and
get your food already!

Milton was livid. That was the last straw. He was finally going to teach these kids a lesson.

Milton turned his head, but before he could get a peep out, a plastic cup full of water smacked him directly in the face.

MILTON
God damnit!

The teenagers in the car behind me all laughed.

HIGH SCHOOL GUY

Look, you got him all wet! Ha!

Together, they began to chant.

HIGH SCHOOL KIDS

Water boy! Water boy! Water boy! Water boy!

Milton glanced up and could still see the beautiful Chattanooga employee looking at me. He didn't want to lose my cool in front of her so he simply wiped his forehead and laughed it off. Yet, before anything else could go down, Victor returned with the order.

VICTOR

Here you go, Caballero. Order for Fuda!

MILTON

Yes, muchas gracias, señor.

Milton continued to wipe his brow as he received the bag of food.

Milton peered my head around Victor's side and looked for the beautiful Chattanooga employee one last time. To his dismay, she was gone and it was time to move head.

HONK! HONK!

HIGH SCHOOL GUY

C'mon let's go!

Milton looked in his rearview mirror and gave the kid a death stare.

VICTOR

Is everything OK, Caballero?

MILTON

Yes, Victor, thanks again, see you next time.

Milton finally pulled away, exiting the parking lot wet and humiliated.

HIGH SCHOOL GUY

What a loser!

Victor shook his head, feeling as if Milton should have stuck up for himself against those obnoxious teenagers.

ROAD SCENE - 5 - ON ROUTE TO DESTINATION 2 - EXT.

ROAD SCENE - 5 - ON ROUTE TO DESTINATION 2 - EXT.

With disgust written all over his face, Milton was finally on his way to deliver the food. Milton headed north past Laurel Valley and traveled eight minutes up Glen Cove Road to the bordering town of Bayville, a nice Long Island beach community filled with friendly bars and restaurants.

When Milton drove off the main strip and entered his client's neighborhood, he could tell this was a richer side of the beach community. Every house

Milton passed was a mansion as he continued down the sideroads of Glen Cove. Milton looked at his GPS app and noticed he was one mansion away from his destination. 42 Kilgore Drive was the address. He noticed a small sign that read, "42" placed near the drop off location's entrance gate.

DESTINATION 2 - MOB BOSS MANSION - EXT.

DESTINATION 2 - MOB BOSS MANSION - EXT.

When Milton pulled up to the gate, the gate slowly began to automatically open.

Milton slowly drove up the long driveway lined with lights and neatly hedged bushes. He continued towards a circled-cobble-stoned area located near the front door stoop. Milton parked his car next to the fountain in the middle of the circle and stepped out of the car with the food in-hand. He looked up at the fountain which had a statue of a man riding a horse holding a sword above his head.

MILTON

Hmm, interesting...

Milton continued his way up to the front door, though before he could drop off the food, a small man popped out of the shadows.

UPKA

Who are you?

MILTON

Holy shoot! Sorry, sir. I didn't
see you there. I'm with Food Dash.
Order for Fuda.

Milton placed the food next to him on the ground. The man slowly hovered over the food.

UPKA

What is this?

His Russian accent was thick, yet his tone was subtle.

MILTON

This is 42 Kilgore Drive, correct?

The Russian man curiously touched the bag with his toe.

UPKA

Yes, but what is this?

MILTON

It's your food. Someone by the name, Fuda, ordered it.

He remained quiet. The silence made the moment awkward.

UPKA

Food Dash?

MILTON

Here, let me show you the order info.

Milton pulled up the order and turned his phone to show him. Suddenly, without Milton ever guessing that this would happen, his good friend Ramijan sent a text that read:

RAMIJAN'S TEXT

Yo, playa! Transaction complete! Just sold 200 grand of Ethereum to that Russian fool! Come on over, son. It's worth is

going down as we speak! So glad I
sold that shoot! Come on ova, playa!
We gonna party like it's 1999!

Without making any connection that this man could in fact be the Russian investor that Ramijan just hustled, Milton switched the text message back to the Food Dash app.

MILTON

See this is your order.

A moment of silence ensued.

MILTON

Alright, so... I think I'm done here.

The man's eyes blossomed wide with fury. Milton had no idea why at the time, so he just quietly backed away.

UPKA

Thank you, kind young man.
My daughter will be very grateful
for your service.

The Russian man grunted under his teeth, trying to hold in his temper. He quickly grabbed the food and slid through the front door that stood behind him. Milton remained dumbfounded and continued to his car. Milton completed the task on the app and confirmed that he handed the package to the customer. He then hopped back into his car and pulled out his keys. Though, as he started the car, he looked up and could see a beautiful blonde young lady standing in the lit window. She was wearing white lingerie and combing her hair.

MILTON

Fuda!

She was gorgeous. Milton was paralyzed and continued to watch with his mouth wide open. Slowly she removed her bra.

MILTON

Oh my God!

Milton couldn't believe his eyes as she stood there half naked. Milton looked to see if anyone had been near his car, but no one was around and he was in the dark, under some large giant fountain statue. The old man at the door appeared to be gone as well. Milton continued to look around to see if anyone was watching. There was no one in sight. Milton quickly remembered that he had his binoculars in his glove compartment and eagerly reached for them. The vibrations of heaven suddenly came alive as he continued to watch the beautiful free show before his eyes.

MILTON

Oooooo....Ooooo.

Fuda charismatically began to sexually dance in front of the window.

MILTON

Yes! Dance, Fuda! Dance! (Whispering.)

Without Milton noticing, his seat's heating pad plugged into his cigarette lighter began to spark. To his dismay, one of the sparks landed on his Food-Hub delivery bag.

MILTON

What's happening! What's that smell?

To his surprise, smoke emitted from the Food-Hub bag resting in Milton's lap. Milton quickly looked down at the newly flamed bag.

MILTON

This can't be good!

Milton quickly lowered the window and tried to throw it out the window, but the bag was stuck in the seatbelt. Suddenly, the flame grew bigger.

MILTON

Oh my god!

The bag became more and more difficult to hold. Milton now started to scream.

MILTON

Ouch! Ouch!

The young lady in the window heard Milton from the driveway and quickly covered herself. She ran behind the curtain and looked right at him.

MILTON

Shoot! She saw me! I gotta get out of here!

Fuda could see the flames inside Milton's car and, with fear, ran away from the window. Milton thankfully managed to toss the burnt bag outside the window.

The front entranceway light kicked back on.

MILTON

Damnit !

It was the small man with his daughter behind him; only this time, she was dressed in a night robe. Milton made eye contact with him as he glazed back at him with fire in his eyes.

MILTON
Shoot, shoot, shoot!

Milton drove his car in reverse and took out the first three hedges behind him. The gate started to close as well, which Milton, without knowing, plowed completely through. He then threw a screeching u-turn and peeled away.

With his eyes opened wide, Milton looked into the rearview mirror and could see the large mansion getting smaller and smaller as he drove further and further away.

MILTON
Holy shoot, holy shoot! Holy shoot!

The small Russian man walked closer to the burning bag on the ground.

FUDA
Papa, what is it?

UPKA

Nothing lipshkin, go back inside. Papa will take care of it.

He extinguished the burning bag with his shoe and examined it. He then pulled out a tiny flipphone from his inside jacket and dialed a number.

BORIS

Yea, boss?

UPKA

I zink we have a problem.

BORIS

Problem boss?

UPKA

It seems as if our friend, Ramijan, has scammed us?

BORIS

Scammed us boss?

UPKA

Yes! Could you stop repeating everything I'm saying!

BORIS

Sorry, Boss!

UPKA

Now listen very carefully, Boris. I want you to follow a Nissan Sentra with license plates FHS432. He's heading southbound on Tom Cove Road. Hurry up and find that car. The driver must be his assistant. I want you to take him for ransom. Then ve vill have another little chat with our good friend Ramijan. This vill teach that young American prick to mess with me!

BORIS

Yes, boss. I'll get right on it.

UPKA

Good, Boris. And no stops to the Doughnut Palace! I've got 200 grand on the line here!

CLICK!

ROAD SCENE - 6 - ON ROUTE TO DINER - EXT.

ROAD SCENE - 6 - ON ROUTE TO DINER - EXT.

MILTON

Great! Just Great! There goes my job as a Food Dasher! It'll be back to the storefront at the BSV Pharmacy where I'll be taking shoot from the elderly with all their daily discount coupons and sales on probiotic pills!

When Milton made it back to the light by Chattanooga's, he noticed my phone was giving me an alert. It was the Food Dash app with another trip.

MILTON

I guess I better accept this and make money while I can. It won't be long before I get fired for leaving burning delivery bags on people's driveways and busting through their million dollar gates.

Milton looked at the app and it offered to pick up an order from their local diner called:

The Green-House Diner

The traffic light turned green and Milton drove straight towards the diner. Behind, however, was the Russian's henchmen, Boris and Vladimir, who finally found me.

BORIS

Look there he is!

The henchmen gained closer on Milton's tail.

VLADIMIR

He's going to the diner! Keep after him!

Carefully, the two followed Milton into the parking lot, trying their best not to be recognized by anyone.

CHAPTER 15

DINER - INT.

DINER - INT.

Milton, still unaware that he was now being tailed, hopped out of the car and walked into the diner. Milton informed the hostess that he was a Food Dasher.

DINER HOSTESS

What's the name?

MILTON

Uh, Ashley.

DINER HOSTESS

Alright, it'll be ready in one sec.

MILTON

OK, thanks.

Milton stepped to the side and found a bench to sit on in the waiting area. For the first two minutes, he glanced through   pictures on his phone. A minute or two later, Milton looked up and the food still wasn't ready.

MILTON

Well, it seems as if I still have
a few minutes here. Might as well
play a quick round of blitz chess
on my phone.

After a minute of playing chess, Milton looked up to see if the food was ready. It was still being prepared. He then stood to his feet to stretch his legs and walked back near the diner's front cash register. Milton looked at the Friday night crowd and noticed the usual group. There were some late-night-daters, teenagers hanging out, and a few older people rebelling against the early bird special.

Though there was one table with two guys, who were suspiciously staring at Milton. Milton straightened his relaxed position on the edge of the counter and lowered one brow.

The two men quickly turned away as if they caught Milton looking at them.

The hostess finally walked towards Milton with a plastic bag full of delicious diner food.

DINER HOSTESS

Pick up for Ashley?

MILTON

Yup, that's me!

DINER HOSTESS

Alright, here ya go. Have a good one.

MILTON

Yea, you too.

HENCHMEN IN VAN BEHIND SIGN - EXT.

HENCHMEN IN VAN BEHIND SIGN - EXT.

BORIS

Yes, boss!

All Boris could hear was a dial tone.

VLADIMIR

What did he say?

Vladimir was sitting in the passenger seat next to Boris.

BORIS

He wants us to follow a Nissan Sentra with this license plate. Says we got to hi-jack the driver and use him for ransom.

VLADIMIR

Ransom?

BORIS

Yeah. Says he's connected to the bit-coin-trader boss was dealing with earlier. Says the guy scammed him out of 200 grand.

VLADIMIR

Scammed him?

BORIS

Would you stop repeating everything I say!

VLADIMIR

Sorry.

BORIS

C'mon let's go. Get your ski mask ready. We got a driver to catch.

VLADIMIR

Can we go to Doughnut Palace, before we start?

BORIS

No, boss says we got to find this guy right away. We'll come back after we snatch the guy.

Vladimir nodded in agreement.

The two henchmen in their white van pulled away from their hiding spot behind a large Chattanooga's billboard-sign located near the Tom Cove train station. They were now in search of me, thinking I was all a part of Ramijan's witty bit-coin trade.

ROAD SCENE - 7 - TAILED BY HENCHMEN - ON ROUTE TO DESTINATION 3 - EXT.

ROAD SCENE - 7 - TAILED BY HENCHMEN - ON ROUTE TO DESTINATION 3 - EXT.

On Milton's way out, he turned back around to see if the two suspicious men were still watching him. To Milton's surprise, they were suddenly gone. Milton thought it was strange, but didn't think much of it, so he continued on to his car as if everything was fine.

When Milton made it back to his Nissan Sentra, he fumbled around for his keys. After Milton eventually found them, he opened his car door and placed the food on the passenger seat. Milton then confirmed with the Food Dash app that he had the food and started the engine.

At last, Milton finally made his way out of the parking lot.

Without Milton ever knowing, the white van, with the two Russian henchmen, quietly rolled out of the parking lot and continued to follow him.

Moving ahead, Milton received the directions for his next drop off. The app routed the trip back to Roslyn, an eight minute drive, which wasn't too bad.

Returning to the light by Chattanooga's, Milton fumbled with the radio app and searched for some tunes to play. Milton suspiciously glanced in his rear-view mirror and noticed the white van was stopped one car behind him. Now, Milton normally wouldn't have thought anything of it, but in this case, he noticed one of the suspicious characters from the diner driving the car. Milton could tell it was him because he noticed the henchman's ponytail. To his right, was the other larger man Milton recently spotted in the diner as well.

MILTON

Are they following me? No, you're just getting paranoid.

Milton continued to play with the radio app, but still felt a bit concerned. He again looked into the rearview mirror and noticed the men continuing to look straight ahead at his car. The light, however, finally turned green. Milton ignored the thought of being followed and continued ahead through the light.

A bit down the road, Milton could still see the van close behind. He tried to drive a bit faster to get away from them, but the van stayed suspiciously close. Milton flipped his directional on and changed lanes, thinking this would shake them off his tail. Milton looked back in his side view mirror and could see the van switching lanes as well. Now, he was beginning to grow worried. Milton sped up and passed an old beat up truck on his right-hand side and sharply re-entered the right lane. The van was persistent and followed Milton into the right-hand lane shortly after.

MILTON

What the hell's going on?

Milton continued to swerve in and out of the next two cars ahead of him, but the van wouldn't give up in their pursuit after him. Luckily, the GPS informed me to make the next right, which Milton was thankful for. Milton safely made the turn and looked back to see if the van had followed him. The van, on the other hand, continued to drive straight down the main road.

MILTON

They're gone. This night keeps getting stranger and stranger.

EMPTY PARKING LOT NEAR PORT - EXT.

EMPTY PARKING LOT NEAR PORT - EXT.

Milton shook off the recent chase and continued with the delivery. After a few turns down the inner side streets of Roslyn, he somehow found himself in an empty parking lot by the Roslyn Harbor. Milton parked my car and checked the app.

MILTON

This can't be right.

There was no one around except for the lonely low tide that filled Milton's senses. The moon hung brightly above the water and all he could see were the shadows of the old wooden pier that rested in the harbor's shallow waters.

Knowing something was wrong, Milton texted the client:

MILTON'S TEXT

Hi, this is your Food Dasher. The GPS brought me to 24 Seaside Lane, Rosevale. I don't see a 24 around here at all. In fact, I don't see anything but the harbor. Can you help me out?

Milton could see she read the message.

CUSTOMER'S TEXT

Oh, I'm sorry, this always happens. It's actually 24 Seaside Lane, Rosevale Heights. So sorry about the confusion.

MILTON

I knew it!

Milton continued to text her:

MILTON'S TEXT

Alright, no problem, I'll be there soon.

CUSTOMER'S TEXT

So sorry about the confusion. Thanks again.

MILTON'S TEXT

No problem.

MILTON

Damnit!

Milton turned the car back on. His back began to bother him and the sciatic pain he always felt after the first few drop offs started to kick in. To make matters worse, Milton could see something bright approaching me.

MILTON

Who the hell could be here at this time of night, I asked myself.

Milton looked in his rearview mirror and to his dismay, it was the white van that had been following him from before. Milton's eyes grew wide with fear.

MILTON

Oh, shoot! Not these guys again!

The van was now parked directly behind him. They flipped on their car's brights, which really frightened Milton. Milton quickly fumbled for his keys and nervously managed to get the key inside the ignition. Though before Milton could place the car in drive, a loud tap could be heard on his window. Milton looked to his left and noticed the long ponytailed man pointing a handgun at him.

VLADIMIR

Get out of the car!

Milton raised his left hand and shut off the engine with the other. At this point, Milton was terrified. Even after all the shoot he'd been through already, this was really the first time Milton feared for my life.

VLADIMIR

Get out of the damn car!

Milton unlocked the car door and slowly stepped out of the car.

MILTON

Listen, man, whatever I did to
you guys, I'm sure we can settle
this, I...

But before Milton could get another word out,
in came the heavy set man with a cloth bag, that
he quickly slid over Milton's head. The other man
grabbed Milton's hands and tied them together with
a rope behind his back. Milton moved his head
around, trying to free himself.

MILTON

Listen, we can work this out!

BORIS

Stop moving around you idiot!
C'mon Vlad, help me get him in
the back of the van.

MILTON

What! Wait! Where are you
taking me!

The larger man lifted my head-covering and
slapped a piece of duct tape over my mouth.

BORIS

I said, shut the damnit up!
C'mon Vlad, get ze damnit ing
door open!

He forcefully escorted Milton into the back of the van. Suddenly, my phone began to ring in my pocket.

VLADIMIR

What is that?

BORIS

It's his damn phone, you idiot.
Hurry, hurry! Get it! Get it!
Vladimir pulled the phone out of my pocket and noticed it was Ramijan.

VLADIMIR

Who is dis Ramijan?
Boris grabbed the phone out of Vladimir's hand and answered the call.

BORIS

We have your man!

RAMIJAN

Huh?

BORIS

We have your man!

RAMIJAN

Mil, you whack son? What you be doin'? You comin' over soon?

The boys just got here. They already hit the bong and we're gettin' ready to play Battle Warfare.

In the background, you can hear Ramijan's mom, in a thick, Indian accent.

RAMIJAN'S MOM

Rami! I smell smoke! You better not be smoking anything down there!

RAMIJAN

It's nothing mom! It's just incents! Sorry, playa, what were you sayin?

BORIS

We have your man! If you don't give us back the money, we will shoot your friend in ze head!

RAMIJAN

Uh...

PARKER

Hey, Rami, who are you talkin' to? Hurry up and get back in

the game. You already missed the first skirmish!

Ramijan, however, suddenly felt less lighthearted as he now realized who he might be talking to.

RAMIJAN

Listen, man. I'll give you back the money; whatever you want. Just don't hurt my friend. He's not a part of this.

BORIS

A part of it or not, your friend will be dead if you don't do as we say. Our boss is very pissed off at you!"

RAMIJAN

Alright, alright, uh, just tell me where you want me to meet you and I'll square off everything. Just, please, don't hurt my friend.

BORIS

Meet us at the warehouse by the Port Wallington pier at midnight. If you don't show up, your friend will be dead in ze water!

Click!

RAMIJAN'S BASEMENT - INT.

RAMIJAN'S BASEMENT - INT.

Ramijan removed his mobile phone away from his ear and stared at it in a daze.

RAMIJAN
Oh shoot.

BENSON
Who was that, Rami?

RAMIJAN
Oh, shoot!

Parker and Benson paused their Battle Warfare game and looked at each other with confusion.

BENSON

Rami, who just called you?

RAMIJAN

The Russian mafia.

PARKER

Ha, for real, Rami, who was that?

RAMIJAN

Seriously, the Russian mafia.

PARKER

Stop playin' Rami.

RAMIJAN

I'm not joking. They have Milton.

Benson and Parker slowly stood from their gaming chairs.

BENSON

Rami, what did you get yourself into?

RAMIJAN

Well, remember how I got into bit-coin and all that?

BENSON AND PARKER
Yea...

RAMIJAN
Well, I kinda sold a bunch of Ethereum to a Russian Investor.

BENSON
OK... and...

RAMIJAN
And... that's it. Really, I did everything by the books. The trade was all legal.

BENSON
So, what would they want with Milton?

RAMIJAN
Well, the value of the Ethereum was predicted to go down and...

PARKER
And...

RAMIJAN

And I did relay that information to Milton earlier.
Ramijan paused.

RAMIJAN

Oh, no!

BENSON

What! What's, oh no?

RAMIJAN

The Russians, they must have intercepted the text I sent to Milton earlier. I told him how the value of the Ethereum was going to go down!

PARKER

And you think they tracked that message down?

RAMIJAN

It's highly unlikely, but it could have happened.

BENSON

Alright, well, whatever happened, we have to call the police.

RAMIJAN

No! No police!

BENSON

What? Why?

RAMIJAN

If my mom finds out I was selling Ethereum to the Russian Mafia, she'd kill me.

PARKER

If we don't act now, the Russian Mafia will kill Milton.

Ramijan paced around the room with his hands over his head.

RAMIJAN

Let me just think for a minute!

BENSON

Dude, what do you have to think about, this is the Russian mob, we have to call the police!

Ramijan continued to walk back and forth nervously in his basement. He then noticed the Battle

Warfare game still playing in the background and suddenly had an idea.

RAMIJAN

Wait! I got it!

BENSON

Huh?

RAMIJAN

I got it. I got an idea!

Ramijan walked to the nearby wall closet and found himself digging through a large pile of storage items.

RAMIJAN

Aha!

Ramijan's body was half way inside the closet. Benson and Parker rolled their eyes, thinking the same thing. Ramijan, however, excitedly pulled out three paintball guns

RAMIJAN

C'mon boys, this means war!

BENSON

What, are you crazy! You want three average guys with paintball guns to battle the Russian Mob. Are you insane!

RAMIJAN

C'mon, you know how we're always saying how cool it would be to fight in a real life battle. Well boys, here's our chance.

PARKER

Yea, we were clearly delusional and not thinking about, you know, getting shot in the face!

RAMIJAN

C'mon, stop being such pussies. No one's really going to shoot anyone. You'll just be... my backup!

BENSON

Backup? Rami, you've officially lost it. This is way too over our heads.

RAMIJAN

Suit it yourselves boys, It's either the tough get going, or the goin' gets tough!

PARKER

Well, which one is it?

BENSON

I'm not sure. Anyway, never mind that. C'mon! We gotta save Milton! Are you in?

Benson and Parker looked at each other both thinking, *this is really a bad idea,* yet, they both noticed the sincerity in his eyes. Ramijan needed his friend's help and so did Milton. Parker looked back at Benson.

PARKER

I lived a good life. Rami, I'm in!
Ramijan gave Parker a paintball gun as he stood by Ramijan's side.

RAMIJAN

Benson?

BENSON

You guys are crazy. I'm calling the cops.

RAMIJAN

Fine, do what you gotta do. Parker, we gotta leave now if we want to make it to the pier on time. We only have 25 minutes to get there.

PARKER

Right!

The two left eagerly, but left Benson behind. Benson dialed 911 on his phone. A dial tone could be heard.

911 OPERATOR

911, what's the emergency, sir?

BENSON

This is, uh, er, uh, Detective Murphopolous. I'm with a local undercover unit. There's going to be a big shootout down at the Port Wallington piers at midnight! I need backup asap!

Benson quickly ended the call. He looked up and noticed he was alone. Without mulling it over anymore, the third member of the Milton rescue squad caved in and decided to join the others.

BENSON

Guys? Guys? Oh, damnit ! Guys!
Wait up for me!

ROAD SCENE - 8 - BORIS' VAN - INT.

ROAD SCENE - 8 - BORIS' VAN - INT.

So there I was, sitting in the back of some creepy van with a bag over my head. I tried to kick and scream, but no one could hear me.

BORIS
Shut ze damnit up back there!
Boris as he slammed the van's divider-wall behind him.

BORIS

Dis damn guy!

Boris continued to drive. He then looked to his right and could see his partner, Vladimir, eating French fries out of a tin tray.

BORIS

What ze damnit are you doing?

VLADIMIR

What? I'm eating.

Vladimir's mouth was full of fries.

BORIS

When ze hell did you manage to get food?

VLADIMIR

Before.

BORIS

When before?

VLADIMIR

Before we got back in ze van, I saw a bag of food sitting in the guy's passenger seat. I was hungry, so I grabbed it.

BORIS

How can you think of food at a time like this! We are working, you idiot!

VLADIMIR

Geez, I'm sorry. I was hungry.

A moment of silence ensued.

VLADIMIR

You want ze French fry?

Boris paused. He could smell the delicious fried crispy potato lingering on the fries.

BORIS

They do smell tasty.

He couldn't resist.

BORIS

OK, gimme one, but just one.

Vladimir held the tin tray next to Boris. Boris plucked out a fry and put it in his mouth.

BORIS

Hmm, yes, zis is good. Very good!

VLADIMIR

Ha! I knew you would like it.
You act like angry bear, but when
you eat ze French fry, you become
as happy as a kitten!

Milton could smell the fries. He continued to scream, hoping someone would hear him along the way to the warehouse.
Boris knocked on the wall again.

BORIS

I said, shut up back there!

Boris' mouth was full of fries. The two looked at each other and laughed.

BORIS

These American French-fries
are really good! But are they American or French?

Vladimir shrugged his shoulders.

VLADIMIR

Hear, you want to try a piece of this.

BORIS

What is it?

VLADIMIR
It's called Philly Cheesesteak!
Here, you try!

Vladimir ripped off a piece of the hero and handed it to his partner. Boris took a bite and immediately was in heaven.

BORIS
Wow, what is this Philly Cheesesteak? I must have more!

VLADIMIR
Ha, you see! You listen to Vladimir and everything will be OK!

BORIS
Ha! Dis is really good!

Milton screamed again. The two Russians laughed and ignored him as they merrily enjoyed their stolen food, approaching closer and closer towards the warehouse.

ROAD SCENE - 9 - RAMIJAN'S MOTHER'S CAR - INT.

ROAD SCENE - 9 - RAMIJAN'S MOTHER'S CAR - INT.

Benson, Parker, and Ramijan quickly made their way to the warehouse in Ramijan's mother's 2020 Red Toyota Corolla.

PARKER

Step on it, Rami!

RAMIJAN

I'm going as fast as I can! This car wasn't exactly made for special op missions!

BENSON
Here, maybe this will make us feel more like special force agents.

Benson, in the passenger seat, hooked up his mobile device to the car and opened his playlist on his music app.

Unexpectedly, Barry Manilow's "I can't smile without you" played on the radio.

RAMIJAN
Barry freaking Manilow?

BENSON
Shoot, er, uh, sorry, my mom must have gotten a hold of my app. Sorry, let's try this!

Now, the Bee Gee's could be heard playing their popular hit, "How deep is your love".

PARKER
Dude.

BENSON

Sorry. Alright here we go!

On the third try, Benson finally got it as AC/DC's "Highway to hell" came on.

PARKER

Alright, now we're talking! So Rami, what's the plan?

RAMIJAN

So I was thinking, when we get there, we split up. Benson you hide on my right, and Parker you hide on my left. I'll present the Russian's with the flash drive. If they don't release Milton, then that's when we'll open fire. Got it?

PARKER AND BENSON

Got it!

PARKER

And then what?

RAMIJAN

Then we hope we make it out of there alive. Preferably with Milton.

BENSON

Well that sounds reassuring.

RAMIJAN

Look, there's the warehouse! We'll park here; that way no one can see us entering the ground.

The car rolled up to the warehouse parking lot.

PARKER

Good idea.

Ramijan pulled the car over and parked next to an abandoned building near the warehouse. Quietly, he turned the car off.

RAMIJAN

Alright boys, today, we become men.

BENSON

But we already are men.

RAMIJAN

Well, tonight we become real men. Men who can kick some serious ass!

He handed them their paint guns and stepped out of the car. Benson was the last to exit the car.

BENSON

Yup, we're definitely going to die tonight."

WAREHOUSE - 2 - EXT.

WAREHOUSE - 2 - EXT.

BORIS

Come on, Vlad, let's get this guy into the warehouse. Boss is already there waiting for us.

VLADIMIR

Right.

The two Russian mobsters pulled Milton out from the back of the van and walked him inside. At this point, Milton still had no idea where he was. Milton was terrified.

MILTON

So wow, this is how I'm going to die. Great. Just great.

WAREHOUSE - 3 - INT.

WAREHOUSE - 3 - INT.

Anyway, fast forward fifteen minutes from now and Milton is right about at the point of the story where, oh yeah, he was about to get his balls sawed off.

Vladimir slapped the duct tape back over Milton's mouth and Boris slowly approached him with the chainsaw. Luckily, to my good fortune, the sound of a door burst open. The rays from the outside lights quickly filtered through the warehouse's dark room. The Russians all covered their eyes trying to see who had entered the warehouse.

BORIS

Who ze damnit is that?

Boris quickly turned off the chainsaw. Milton turned his head and could see it was Ramijan. Milton tried to say something through the duct tape over his mouth, but could only make out a high pitched squeak.

RAMIJAN

Fear not, Milton. Ramijan is here to save you!

Ramijan calmly remained by the warehouses' entrance doorway. He had a paint gun in one hand and a flash drive in the other. Parker and Benson quietly moved to their positions on either side of the warehouse. They remained undetected by the Russians who were still focused on Ramijan's entrance.

Ramijan took another step closer.

RAMIJAN

Mr. Upka. I have here a flash drive containing all the information you need in order to refund the Ethereum you purchased from me. Now, let our friend go and let's pretend none of this ever happened.

UPKA

Ha, Mr. Ramijan. You make me laugh. You really do. But answer me this, what makes you think I'll give up your friend so easily?

RAMIJAN

Because I believe you to be a man of fair business ethics, Upka. I give you the flash drive and you give me my friend. Let's not complicate this anymore than it already needs to be.

UPKA

Ha, you young fool. You have lots to learn. Can't you see, I have ze upper hand. I don't need your worthless Ethereum; but you, Mr. Ramijan, need your friend.

RAMIJAN

Need? I don't need that whiny bitch! Last thing I need is to hear his mamma callin' me up and blamin' me for his death. shoot!

UPKA

Ha, I find that hard to believe.

Ramijan looked around, seeing if Parker and Benson were in their positions. Upka noticed Ramijan looking around and quickly became paranoid. Ramijan noticed the Russian's concern.

RAMIJAN

Alright, Upka, what do you want?

UPKA

I want all the Ethereum and bit-coin you have!"

RAMIJAN

No way, Upka! Take the flash drive or get nothing!

UPKA

Mr. Ramijan, I'm in no mood for negotiations." Upka signaled Boris to raise his gun at my head. "This is your last warning. Either give me your Ethereum, or this young man gets a bullet lodged in his head.

Ramijan paused to think about the situation.

MILTON

Rami, what are you think-
ing about! Give him the damn
Ethereum!

Boris stepped closer towards Milton, raising the gun an inch away from his forehead.

RAMIJAN

Alright! Alright! It's yours. All
of it!

Upka signaled Boris to lower his gun. The Russian henchman followed his boss' orders and stepped away from Milton. Milton almost shoot himself at that point.

UPKA

The flash drive! Toss it to me!

Ramijan looked to his left and then to his right, preparing himself to signal Parker and Benson to open fire. Upka, on the other hand, caught Ramijan looking around.

UPKA

We're not alone, men.

RAMIJAN

Ha, what do you mean?

UPKA

The flash drive, God damnit!
Toss me ze damnit ing flash drive!

Ramijan was running out of options. He slid the flash drive towards the Russian's glossy shoes.

RAMIJAN

Now release the hostage!

UPKA

Temper, temper, young man!
You'll get your friend back when you've sent me all your coin!

RAMIJAN

That wasn't the deal, Upka!

UPKA

Vell, vell, vell; it doesn't look like you have a say in ze matter now, does it?

RAMIJAN

Ah - damnit this shoot! Gents, now's the time! Let's light these assholes up!"

On cue, Parker and Benson stood out from the crates and opened fire on the Russians.

PARKER

Eat paintball shoot, you Russian mobster dicks!

Benson rolled out from the box he was hiding behind and fired a round of paintballs directly into Vladimir's nuts.

BENSON

Yea! Nards shot! Ten points!

The Russians quickly covered their heads and started to retreat. Upka lowered himself to the ground and noticed his men scrambling around the warehouse, looking for cover.

UPKA

You idiots! What are you doing! They're just little balls of paint!

VLADIMIR

Dees little balls of paint hurt!
Ouch!

UPKA

You have ze real zing! Fire back,
you numbskulls!

Boris and Vladimir quickly found cover behind nearby crates and loaded their handguns. Boris was on one side of the warehouse and Vladimir was on the other. Milton was in between them with the small Russian boss cowardly hiding behind me.

RAMIJAN

Keep moving forward!

Ramijan continued to shoot paintballs in their direction. Milton's friends' hopeful attack was quickly countered with return fire.

RAMIJAN

shoot! shoot! Find cover!

Both Parker and Benson quickly jumped behind whatever they could find as a shield. Parker hid behind a nearby forklift and Benson quickly scrambled behind a thick metal beam.

BENSON

Now what!

RAMIJAN

I'm not sure! I didn't plan this far ahead!

PARKER

Rami! These bullets sure seem a lot more frightening in real life!

BENSON

No, shoot! I knew this was a
bad idea!

Upka stood to his feet, feeling a little more confident with his henchmen's use of real ammunition.

UPKA

You see! This is what happens
when you play with ze real men!
Boris and Vladimir continued to fire round after round at Milton's friends.

BENSON

Rami!

Benson tucked himself tightly behind the beam.

RAMIJAN

I'm thinking, I'm thinking!

Suddenly, they heard a big crash from the glass roof above our heads and a big bang through the main entrance door behind them.

POLICE CHIEF

Everybody freeze! This is the Nassau County Police Department!

BENSON

Man am I glad I called these guys!

Upka quickly picked Milton up from the chair and held a gun to the side of his head.

UPKA

I'll blow this young man's head off!

A helicopter spot light swirled around his feet.

POLICE CHIEF

Sir, we have the place surrounded. Surrender now and no one gets hurt!

UPKA

Not a chance, you American scum! Boys, provide me with cover fire!

Both Boris and Vladimir continued to fire as Upka pushed Milton towards the back of the warehouse. The police fired back. Benson and Ramijan quickly crawled behind Parker and covered their ears as the real life shootout ensued. Ramijan peered his eyes around the forklift and could see Upka dragging Milton away.

RAMIJAN

C'mon, he's getting away with Milton!

BENSON

Dude, I think we've done our
part. The police can handle it
from here!

Ramijin remained silent, patiently waiting for a lull in the gunfire. When he found his opportunity, he ran for it, making his way to help Milton. Parker looked at Benson and shrugged his shoulders.

PARKER

Sorry.

Parker quickly followed Ramijan's lead.

BENSON

Wait, no, Parker! Get back here!

A bullet ricocheted off the forklift, scaring Benson back.

BENSON

Oh, damnit ! damnit ! damnit !
Alright, Benson, you can do this!

He then counted to three in his head and ran for it, following his friends to the other side of the warehouse.

PARKER

Ahhh!

A few seconds later, Vladimir and Boris were quickly surrounded by the Special Force Unit and were forced to surrender. Immediately, the police handcuffed the two Russian henchmen.

VLADIMIR

You know, I just love your Philly Cheesesteak!

Boris simply rolled his eyes as the N.C.P.D continued to capture the two. Milton, on the other hand, continued to be pushed by Upka with his gun to the young dasher's head.

WAREHOUSE - 4 - THE DOCKS - EXT.

WAREHOUSE - 4 - THE DOCKS - EXT.

UPKA

Come on, stop dragging your feet!

He pushed Milton through the backdoor of the warehouse and continued to hold the gun to his head. Milton now found himself on an old wooden pier located just behind the warehouse. Upka pointed the gun to a nearby boat docked next to the pier.

UPKA

Hurry, get in ze boat you idiot!

Milton had no choice, but to follow Upka's orders. Milton carefully stepped inside the twenty-footer speedboat. It was quite difficult as his hands were still tied together. The adrenaline somehow gave Milton perfect balance, and as a result, he made it into the boat safely. Upka quickly followed in after Milton and untied the boat from the dock. He then ran to the front of the boat and started its engine. The water behind the boat began to bubble, turning the calm water into a rumbling mixture of saltwater foam.

As we slowly started to pull away from the pier, Milton could see his three friends exiting out of the warehouse's backdoor.

MILTON

Rami!

Milton yelled as their boat moved further and further away from the pier.

UPKA

Shut up!

Ramijan frantically looked around and, perchance, spotted a boat with the key's in its starter.

RAMIJAN

That one! C'mon guys, hop in!

The boat was labeled, "The Rim-job" in elegant cursive font.

BENSON
The Rim-Job?

PARKER
Maybe the owner's a plumber?

BENSON
Or a porn-star? Either or?

RAMIJAN
Never mind, its name! Just hop
in the damn boat!

CHAPTER

25

LONG ISLAND SOUND - BOAT SCENE - EXT.

LONG ISLAND SOUND - BOAT SCENE - EXT.

The three hurriedly jumped in the boat. Benson and Parker untied the boat from the dock while Ramijan started its engine. Slowly, their boat drifted away from the dock. Ramijan wasted no time and pushed the boat's engine into forward drive. Not a moment later, Milton could see their boat's light trailing behind ours. Milton waved his tied hands high in the air, trying to flag them down. Upka turned his head.

UPKA

Agh!! You're friends don't know when to give up!

Upka made a hard turn out of the harbor, now making their way along the coast of the Long Island Sound. Ramijan, Benson, and Parker continued their pursuit. They quickly caught up as their boat was more adapted for racing. But to better Milton's chances of getting rescued, in came the N.C.P.D water-patrol following close behind his friends. In addition, a helicopter's spotlight could be seen guiding their boat as it was a bit difficult to see through the moonlit sound.

Ramijan quickly steered the boat next to Upka. Milton raised his hands in support of their efforts. Now side by side, the two boats raised through the dark waters of the early morning hue. Benson and Parker fired their paintballs, which splattered against the side of the boat.

RAMIJAN

That's it boys, we got him on the run!

Upka lowered his head, avoiding the oncoming paintball fire. Though, to Milton's friends' dismay, their paintball ammunition suddenly ran out.

PARKER

We're out of fire power!

Upka quickly realized the pause in Milton's friends' firing and grabbed his gun on the boat's dashboard. Immediately, he pointed it at his friends.

RAMIJAN

Get down!

Upka fired four shots at Milton's friends' speed-boat.

UPKA

Ha ha! You zink you can mess
with Upka, you American piece
of sheet!

Tucked low behind the boat's inner wall was Benson and Parker. Ramijan also ducked low behind the steering wheel.

BENSON

Rami, we're screwed!

Ramijan looked around the boat, thinking of a way to stop Upka. Parker, on the other hand, noticed a small container near the short-staircase leading to the bottom cabin. Without wasting any more time, he quickly ran for it. He immediately popped it open and found a box full of sex toys.

PARKER
Hey, guys, I was right, the owner of this boat is a pornstar!

RAMIJAN
Parker, are you crazy, get down!

Upka fired another two shots at the boat, causing Rami to swerve left and right. Parker quickly carried the box of sex toys to Benson.

PARKER
C'mon, we can distract him with these!

BENSON
What, are you nuts?

PARKER
Got a better idea?!

Parker was right, they were running out of options and without another thought given, Benson and Parker started tossing dildos, penis pumps, and butt plugs at the Russian mob boss. Ramijan steered the boat closer to Upka's side and, to their good fortune, the rubber sex toys seemed to be doing the trick.

To Upka's dismay, a long, one and half foot dildo slapped him across the face.

UPKA

Ugh!

MILTON

Alright, boys! You got him good!

This, however, only angered Upka even more. He raised his gun and aimed it at Benson and Parker who were like two sitting ducks in a pond. Milton had to act fast. He was close enough to reach Upka and stop him.

UPKA

Eat led you stupid American sheets!

Desperately, Milton stood from the boat's bench and lowered his shoulder into Upka's side. Upka squeezed the trigger, but the shot was fired straight into the air. They both, however, landed on the boat's steering wheel, which wildly turned into Milton's friends' boat.

Upon impact, Ramijan lost control of the boat as it now headed towards a nearby rock-filled jetty. Their boat skidded over the jetty, sending it and all three of Milton's friends into the air.

PARKER, BENSON, and RAMIJAN
Whoooaaa!

They soared high through the early morning sky.
SPLASH!

Luckily, the N.C.P.D were close behind to rescue them.

Milton, on the other hand, was quickly thrown to the ground by Upka.

He turned around and noticed his friends' boat capsized, floating upside down.

UPKA
Ha! You see! That's what happens when you mess with me!

Milton also looked back and could see the cap-sized boat now surrounded by a rescue team of coast guards and police officers. Milton was worried about his friends. But his worry turned into hate for the mad-man who stood before him.

MILTON
You...

UPKA
You what?

Upka continued to drive the boat down the coast.

MILTON

You...ASSHOLE!

Milton slowly stood to his feet again. He desperately wanted to hurt this mad-man for what he did to his friends. It was difficult to stand in the boat, but Milton slowly made his way to the front. Though, he didn't get very far as Upka turned around and noticed Milton creeping up. Upka held his gun to Milton's chest.

UPKA

I told you to sit down!

Milton didn't care. He was furious with rage and hate. Milton held his ground and stood there.

The boat hit a rock, making Upka lose control of the boat for a second. Milton fell to one knee. He quickly gained control of the boat and continued to drive forward.

He turned around again and noticed Milton standing back to his feet.

UPKA

God damnit, I said sit down!

The shore was approaching closer and closer. Milton slowly took another step. Upka was clumsily trying to steer the boat and simultaneously pointing the gun in Milton's direction.

UPKA

One more step and I blow your
brains out, you American piece of
sheet!

I looked over his shoulder and could see another jetty approaching.

MILTON

Think again, you asshole!

Upka noticed Milton looking ahead and quickly turned his eyes forward. But before he could get a chance to steer clear of the jetty, the front of the boat hit a rock and, like Milton's friends' boat, went airborne. Though, unlike their boat, Upka and Milton's boat had been closer to the shore, which ultimately skidded along the sanded coast of Port Washington.

CHAPTER

26

SHORE SCENE - EXT.

SHORE SCENE - EXT.

When the boat landed, Milton was thrown towards the back of the boat. He lost consciousness and blacked out upon impact. Upka managed to hold onto the steering wheel and managed to survive the crash-landing unscathed. A bit shaken up, but overall able to continue making his escape from the oncoming N.C.P.D who proceeded with their pursuit.

Upka looked back and noticed Milton was knocked out. He grumbled and figured Milton was no use anymore. The Russian boss held his arm in a bit of pain, but managed to hop out of the boat and land on both feet into the soft sand in which the boat now rested.

Upka looked back and could see the swirling lights of the police force coming his way. The helicopter's bright spotlight was also heading for him.

Yet, conveniently, for Upka, the shore was located next to a busy part of town filled with shops, restaurants, and bars. The Russian hurtled over the guard railing and found himself onto the main street. The helicopter, however, quickly caught up to him and shone its spotlight directly over his head. He looked up and covered his eyes, looking back at the helicopter. Without giving it another thought, he gave the N.C.P.D helicopter pilot the middle finger and quickly continued to run towards the main part of town.

Milton, on the other hand, began to wake up from his unconscious state. He stood to his feet and could see the helicopter swarming around the main street nearby. Milton quickly hopped off the boat and ran to the main street where he could now see Upka making his escape with the bright helicopter spotlight hovering above. The rage inside Milton continued to boil. He couldn't let this mad-man get away.

Milton rubbed the thin ropes binding his hands together against the sharp edge of the guardrail and was able to break free. He then hurtled over the guard rail and continued to chase Upka, who could now be seen entering the other Chattanooga restaurant located here in Port Washington.

Milton hobbled his way across the street, avoiding the early morning traffic as it was now almost 1 a.m.

CHATTANOOGA'S
RESTAURANT - 2 - INT.

CHATTANOOGA'S RESTAURANT - 2 - INT.

The store was still open as most Chattanooga restaurants closed at 2 a.m.

Upka quickly entered the fast-food restaurant, holding his wounded arm with one hand and grasping his gun with the other. The early morning patrons who were there screamed at the very first sight of Upka hobbling into the store. He then waved his gun at the cashier and the workers who were working the late night shift.

UPKA

Nobody move!

The patrons and employees inside the restaurant screamed.

Milton could see him waving his gun around from the outside window. But that didn't stop him from trying to catch this lunatic. The police quickly made their presence, as four cop cars screeched into the Chattanooga's parking lot. Milton quietly sneaked inside the restaurant and laid low behind the closest table near the entranceway. Upka looked desperate. You could see he was running out of options and places to run.

The light from the helicopter could be seen flashing through the restaurant window onto Upka's face. He continued to look around with a mad scowl on his face. He pointed his gun at a group of patrons sitting in a booth. They backed further into the corner of their seats in fear. He then wildly turned his gun to the employees behind the counter. They immediately stopped working and too backed up into the kitchen counters they were preparing the food on just a minute ago.

Upka pointed to a female Chattanooga employee.

UPKA

You!

The girl frighteningly pointed to herself.

UPKA

Yes, you! Come here!

Milton peered his eyes over the booth and could see it was the Chattanooga employee he had a crush on. To her right, Milton could also see Victor. They must have been working the late night shift together at this Port Washington branch.

The scared young female employee slowly stepped closer to Upka.

UPKA

Today, senorita! We don't have all night!

The young girl walked around the counter with tears in her eyes. This enraged Milton even more, but he had to be strategic about his next move. The sounds of the helicopter circling above the restaurant could be heard outside while more and more police cars entered the scene. There was no way out for Upka; or so it appeared.

A police officer could be heard from a loudspeaker above the restaurant.

POLICE CHIEF

I repeat, this is the N.C.P.D Special Force Unit. You are

surrounded. Please surrender and
exit the building with your hands
in the air.

The helicopter continued to circle above the restaurant.

Upka lost his patience and grabbed the girl closer to him. She screamed. He continued to wave his gun at the patrons and employees.

UPKA

Nobody, move or the girl dies!

Upka backed his way with the young lady towards the rear exit of the restaurant. Milton figured the time was now or never, thus, he stepped out from the side of the booth.

MILTON

There's no way out, Upka, it's over!

Upka didn't think twice and pointed the gun at Milton.

MILTON

Oh shoot!

Milton quickly dove back behind the booth. Upka unleashed two shots at me that grazed the booth's pleather seats. The young girl screamed with terror.

CHATTANOOGA BACK PARKING LOT - EXT.

CHATTANOOGA BACK PARKING LOT - EXT.

Aggressively, he continued to drag her out of the restaurant's back door and found himself in the employee parking area.

UPKA

Which one is yours!

The girl continued to scream.

UPKA

Shut up! Which one is yours!

With her finger shaking, she pointed to the nearby Honda Civic.

UPKA

Give me your keys!

She anxiously reached into her jeans pocket and pulled out her keys.

UPKA

Alright, c'mon, get in the car!

Upka forced the young girl into the passenger seat of her own car.

He quickly ran around the front of the car. But before he jumped inside, he looked up at the helicopter that blindly continued to circle above.

UPKA

Ha! Ha! You Stupid Americans!

He then angrily slid into the car and started the engine. Luckily, the car stalled.

UPKA

Ahh! Dis piece of crap!

CHATANOOGA RESTAURANT - 3 - INT.

CHATANOOGA RESTAURANT - 3 - INT.

Back inside the restaurant, Milton peered his eyes over the booth a second time. All he could see were the terrified patrons and employees frozen in fear. Milton quietly snuck around the counter, unsure if the coast was clear. Upka, however, had already left the restaurant. Milton looked around.

MILTON

Is everyone alright?

With fear and tears in their eyes, a couple, with their two young children nodded their heads. The employees appeared to be safe and unharmed as well. Milton glanced his head around the wall and found the back door.

Though, before Milton continued with his pursuit after Upka, Victor threw Milton his keys.

VICTOR

Hey, Caballero, take these. Just
bring it back in one piece, OK?
Milton caught the keys and sighed.

MILTON

Right. Thanks, Victor.

VICTOR

Go save her muchacho!

Milton nodded his head and didn't waste another minute.

CHATTANOOGA EMPLOYEE PARKING LOT - 2 - EXT.

CHATTANOOGA EMPLOYEE PARKING LOT - 2 - EXT.

He burst out of the back door and could see Upka driving away with the young girl in her Honda Civic. Milton quickly pressed the unlock button on Victor's key-fob. When he heard the unlocking beeping of his car, Milton looked to his right and noticed a highly detailed Toyota Hybrid Prius. It was colored purple with thick lightning-decal-artwork on either side of the car.

MILTON

Well, it's better than nothing!

Milton quickly opened the door and hopped into the car. Upon starting the car, he immediately felt the inner hydraulic system lift the entire car while simultaneously playing loud Latino music blaring through the speakers. Milton didn't have time to accommodate my comfort levels and knew he had little time to waste, so he quickly backed out of the parking spot and began his chase after Upka.

ROAD SCENE - 10 - THE UPKA CHASE - EXT.

ROAD SCENE - 10 - THE UPKA CHASE - EXT.

Milton pulled out of the parking lot with the hydraulics in full gear, bouncing the car up and down to loud Reggaetón music. Cars were honking at him left and right as he slowly bounced his way down the main street. Milton guessed correctly and pressed the right button to deactivate the hydraulics. Finally, he started his pursuit on the right foot.

Up ahead Milton could see a car wildly weaving in and out of the few cars up ahead.

MILTON

That has to be him!

Milton applied more pressure to the gas pedal.

Now, it's worth mentioning that only a few hours ago, Milton would have been too scared to chase down one of the world's most feared Russian mobsters. But not now.

The adrenaline was racing through his veins as Milton kept his eye on the prize; and that was to save the girl.

At this point, Milton knew he was surpassing the speed limit; the young dasher had no other option.

Upka looked back in his rear view mirror and could see someone catching up to him quickly. Milton wasn't sure if he knew it was him, but his paranoia kicked in, causing him to drive even faster.

Milton was now two cars behind him. Milton changed lanes and could see Upka diagonally ahead of him.

Upka looked in his rearview mirror and could tell it was Milton. Upka grunted under his breath and continued his reckless driving behavior. He swerved into Milton's right-hand lane and was now one car ahead of Milton.

Milton quickly changed lanes and pulled alongside the car behind Upka. The mad Russian noticed Milton catching up and quickly swerved ahead of him. It caused Milton to hit the brake and swerve a bit. Milton steadied the wheel and regained control of the car.

Milton was still on his tail. He wasn't quite sure what Upka's next move would be, so Milton stuck to him like glue. Ahead, was a ramp to the parkway, which would normally be empty of cars at this early time of the morning.

Upka quickly entered the on-ramp. Milton followed his lead and continued on his tail. They swerved around the clover-leaf and both found themselves racing on the parkway. As Milton predicted, there wasn't any other car in sight. Upka pulled ahead a bit, but Milton drove the Prius as fast as he could. They were both reaching speeds of over 100 miles an hour. At this point, Milton was actually hoping a cop would catch them going over the speed limit; the backup would be appreciated at this point for sure.

They weren't on the parkway for long as Upka quickly decided to drive onto the next exit ramp. His wheels screeched making this hasty move. Milton wasn't too far behind. He too applied the brakes to perform this last minute maneuver. Luckily, Milton pulled it off and followed Upka off the parkway.

Upka looked into his rearview mirror a third time and could see Milton hot on his tail.

UPKA

You young American piece of sheet! Ha!

Milton was about two car lengths behind him and could hear Upka screaming out of the window. Milton, however, stayed focused.

Suddenly, Milton could see Upka's tail lights glowing bright red as he slammed on his brakes. The Russian's car screeched. Milton too was forced to slam on his brakes. Milton turned the steering wheel hard, now swerving around the mad Russian's car.

UPKA

Ha!

Upka continued to laugh out of his window like a madman.

Milton's car continued to slide along the street with smoke coming out of its tires. The young dasher turned his steering wheel left and right trying to regain the stability of his car. Upka continued on my right, driving faster and faster down the dark empty street. Milton finally gained control of the Prius and drove full speed ahead to catch up to Upka.

On either side of the road was acres of Long Island farm land, making the street appear darker and darker. The only light provided was that of the bright moonlight and their headlights that soared down the road.

Upka was now a ways ahead of me. Milton started to feel a sense of doubt, but he didn't want to give up. Milton looked all around the dashboard trying to figure a way to call the police or somehow increase his speed. The young dasher couldn't find anything until he read a button labeled, *"Velocidad"*.

Milton

Huh, what does this mean? Oh
hell, here goes nothing!

When Milton pressed the button, it automatically sent a nitro-boost to the engine, propelling him at an incredible speed.

Milton's head slammed against the back of the head rest.

MILTON

Ahhhh!

And although everything appeared as a light-speed blur, Milton could now see Upka's car approaching closer and closer.

Upka looked into the rearview mirror and could see Milton catching up quickly.

UPKA

What? How?

Within a few seconds, Milton was now racing neck and neck with Upka. The girl screamed inside the car.

FEMALE CHATTANOOGA EMPLOYEE
Help me!

Upka, however, became extremely frustrated. He turned his wheel towards Milton and slammed the side of his car into his. Milton bounced off the road and drove on the dirt and gravel for a bit. Upka unleashed another menacing laugh. Milton, on the other hand, stayed in control and found his way back onto the street.

Again, Milton was side by side with Upka.

The mad Russian turned his wheel towards Milton a second time. Milton learned his lesson though and also turned his wheel outward. They both slammed into each other, only this time, Milton managed to stay on the road. They were both connected side by side, pushing each other's cars back and forth down the dimly lit road.

UPKA
You'll never stop me you Idiot American!

Milton held onto the steering wheel as tight as he could. Though, to his misfortune, Milton heard the sound of a low-tone honk coming from afar. Milton looked up and could now see the lights of an 18 wheeler approaching.

UPKA

Haha! Dis looks like the end
for you, American!

Milton didn't back down. He continued to hold the steering wheel with a firm grip. The truck was coming though, and Milton had to make a decision fast.

Upka continued to laugh like a maniac as the truck neared. The truck-horn honked its low toned honk over and over. The truck driver knew there was no stopping now. Milton looked at the girl in the passenger seat and could see the horror on her face.

Suddenly, something came over Milton. At the last second, with both feet, he slammed onto his brakes and turned the wheel hard into Upka's car. At the last second possible, with perfect timing, Milton managed to bump into Upka's back-right tire and move out of the 18 wheeler's path. The large truck's honking sound quickly vanished into a low toned decrescendo as it continued its way untouched down the road.

Milton's car spun in circles, heading towards the side of the road again. The young dasher's love-tap into Upka's car, however, caused Upka to fishtail from left to right. The mad Russian jarringly steered the wheel back and forth trying to maintain control of his car. Ultimately, he was able to straighten the car out.

Upka looked into the rearview mirror and harked a loud, crazy laugh. The young girl turned in her seat and looked back at my car, spinning out of control.

Finally, Milton's car came to an abrupt stop where he could now see Upka getting away.

The young lady looked at the mad Russian in fear, feeling helpless. She then looked ahead and noticed a family of three deer galloping towards the center of the street.

FEMALE CHATTANOOGA EMPLOYEE
Lookout!

Upka's insidious laugh quickly ended as he opened his eyes wide and immediately tried to swerve out of the way of the deer only 20 yards ahead of them.

At the very last moment, Upka swerved clear of the deer, but as a result, found himself driving on the dirt field adjacent to the street. Again, Upka found himself trying to regain control of the car as the field's terrain was too rough for the young girl's Honda Civic.

In the distance, Milton could still see the car continuing through the field.

Perchance, a pile of dirt lay ahead of Upka and the young girl. The mound was too big and they were driving too fast for Upka to dodge this obstacle.

Upka tried to turn the wheel but it was too late. The car drove straight towards the dirt mound, propelling the car high into the air.

UPKA AND FEMALE CHATTANOOGA EMPLOYEE
AHHhhh!

To make things even more interesting, the car drove straight through a Food Dash billboard, ripping a hole right where the dasher's head was in the picture, leaving a headless young man giving the oncoming drivers an over enthusiastic thumbs up.

The airborne car safely landed. It then spun around in a complete circle and ultimately came to a halt. One of its wheels rolled off and there was smoke coming out of its hood.

MILTON
Holy crap!

Milton started the Prius' engine and dashed towards the totaled car.

FARM FIELD - SIDE OF ROAD - EXT.

FARM FIELD - SIDE Of ROAD - EXT.

He sped up to the scene of the accident and slammed onto the brakes, skidding off the side of the road. Milton hopped out of the car and, without any thought given, ran to see if the young girl was OK.

When Milton approached the passenger side window, he could see the girl was hurt, but still conscious. Upka, however, was out cold, with his head draped over the steering wheel.

The young dasher quickly opened the door and helped her out. He could smell gasoline and the smoke coming out of the hood became thicker and thicker. Milton knew he had to get her out of there fast.

MILTON

Come on. Let's get you out of here.

Milton carefully helped her out of the car.

MILTON

Can you walk?

She painfully nodded her head. Milton could see her leg was badly bruised so he placed his arm under her shoulder to help her walk. They slowly walked back to his car. The gasoline was leaking everywhere and they were running out of time.

MILTON

C'mon, just a bit further.

She arduously nodded her head as Milton helped her limp away from the car. A moment later, they were clear of the scene, but only three-quarters of the way towards the Prius.

Milton and the Chattanooga employee suddenly heard a man's voice.

UPKA

Stop right there you, American, blue jean wearing, jerk!

It was Upka and he was holding his loaded gun. Milton and the Chattanooga employee both froze in shock.

The mad Russian raised his gun and pointed it directly at them.

UPKA

I'll see you in hell, American boy!

Suddenly, the car caught on fire. Upka too noticed the car burning behind him as he felt the heat of the flames hot on his back.

MILTON

I don't think so asshole!

Milton continued to help the young girl towards the car.

MILTON

Get down!

Upka turned around.

UPKA

Uh oh!

Milton and the Chattanooga employee rolled behind the car and covered their ears. Not a second later did the car explode, lifting Upka and the soil he stood upon high into the sky.

UPKA

AHHH!

Upka yelled, soaring like a lit firework into the blue and yellow, early morning sky.

The car again exploded. Milton and the Chattanooga employee held their ears and tucked into each other's body for safety and coverage.

A moment later, Milton peered his head around the front tires of the Prius and could see only a tiny flame burning off the hood of the once intact Honda Civic.

Milton then helped the young girl to her feet.

MILTON

Are you alright?

FEMALE CHATTANOOGA EMPLOYEE

Yea, I think so.

She looked at the burnt automobile before them.

FEMALE CHATTANOOGA EMPLOYEE

Damnit, I just bought that car.

MILTON

Don't worry. I'm sure the insur-
ance will cover you on this one.
There was an awkward moment of silence. The
two both looked down at the ground.

MILTON'S THOUGHTS

*Damnit, even when I'm the hero
I manage to say weird things to
girls.*

The young lady picked her head up.

FEMALE CHATTANOOGA EMPLOYEE

I'm Flora.

MILTON

I'm Milton.

FLORA

Uh... Thanks, for you know,
saving my life and stuff.

MILTON

Yeah, sure, ha, er, uh, no problem.
There was another moment of awkward silence,
which was instantly broken up by the sound of police

sirens making their way closer to the scene. The Nassau County Police Department's SUV's parked along the side of the road. Milton and Flora were both happy to see the police make their presence. Though, to Milton's surprise, out came Benson, Parker and yes, good ol' Ramijan running out of the car.

PARKER

Hey jerk-face! You're alive!

Milton laughed and was relieved to see his friends safe and unharmed. Ramijan had a sling around his arm, but for the most part, they all appeared to be alright.

Immediately, they hugged Milton and presented us with police blankets to keep us warm.

Milton helped Flora wrap a blanket around her.

MILTON

Guys, I'd like to introduce you
to Flora.

She gave Milton's friends an awkward wave.

FLORA

Hi.

PARKER AND BENSON

Hey.

Ramijan, however, found himself hovering over the crisped charcoal body of the burnt Russian mobster.

RAMIJAN

Yup, boys, this one's a goner!
We're going to have to report it to
the chief.

POLICE OFFICER

Who is that kid?

The other police officer standing next to him simply shrugged his shoulders in confusion.

Together they laughed under their breath at Ramijan's continued, yet unofficial participation in the investigation; though, inspired to say the least.

With their blankets still wrapped around them, Milton and his friends took a seat on a nearby wooden guard rail located next to the side of the road.

MILTON

Wow, I can't believe this all just happened.

More police cars and ambulances entered the scene.

BENSON

Looks like we'll be here for a while.

Milton and his friends slowly walked away from the investigation scene.

PARKER
Where are we?

MILTON
Good question.

They all admired the beautiful Long Island farmland around them.

BENSON
Hey, is anyone hungry?

MILTON, PARKER, FLORA
Starving!

BENSON
How about a Food Dash order?
I know a guy who can get us food
real fast!

MILTON
Huh? Wait... Ahhh!

They all laughed at Parker's lame joke; the guy of course referring to Milton.

For the next few moments, Milton and his friends watched the sun make its early morning rise over the Long Island farm-scape, lucky to be alive; lucky to live another day.

(Camera pans away from the scene overhead.)

PICKLEBALL - 2 - EXT.

PICKLEBALL - 2 - EXT.

One Year Later...

So for the most part, after that crazy night of dashing, things have been going pretty well for Milton and friends lately.

They still play pickleball from time to time with good ol' Mr. Barley.

MR. BARLEY
Come on you sissy pansies! Let's see what you got!

The old pickleball-player served the ball.

Like a year ago, Parker slammed the ball into Mr. Barley's head, causing him to go down.

BENSON

Dude, you killed Mr. Barely... Again!

The three quickly ran to his aid and hovered above him. A moment later, his eyes opened wide and a ball of laughter burst from his belly.

MR. BARLEY

Ha! Gotcha!

(Mr. Barley points at them on the ground and the camera freezes on him.)

CHAPTER 34

VIDEO GAME OFFICE - INT.

VIDEO GAME OFFICE - INT.

But otherwise, Benson and Parker left their day time jobs and started working for a video game company. They're currently working on a title called "Dasher Warfare". It's a first person shooter where all the delivery drivers compete in an all out battle to become the world's most feared sharpshooting delivery-man.

POLICE TRAINING
YARD - EXT.

POLICE TRAINING YARD - EXT.

Ramijan finally gained the courage to leave his mom's basement and found an apartment in Brooklyn. He left the bit-coin world and is currently a cadet-in-training with the New York City Police Department. He one day aspires to become lead detective in the N.Y.P.D's International Crime and Investigations Unit.

PAINTBALL FIELD - EXT.

PAINTBALL FIELD - EXT.

In addition, the three friends get together once a year to participate in a New York State paintball competition.

Parker still loves to roll on the ground and shoot his opponents in the groin.

PARKER

Yes! Nard shot!

CHATTANOOGA'S - 4 - DRIVE THRU - EXT.

CHATTANOOGA'S - 4 - DRIVE THRU - EXT.

For Milton, on the other hand, life has been pretty good. He finally left the Food Dashing gig, not that it was bad or anything. Milton just felt like he needed a change, you know, especially after being kidnapped by the Russian mafia and everything. But yea, these days he's currently working at a well known book store called Billy and Nickels. He even finished his first novel. It's kind of a big hit in Milton's small circle at least. The book is about a Food Dasher having the wildest dash of his life.

He appropriately titled it, "The Night Dasher".

And as for his love life, well, Milton's actually been seeing Flora pretty steadily.

Flora still works at Chattanooga's but now serves as their new regional manager, making sure all the local operations are running smoothly. On occasion, Milton and Flora still like to go grab a burger at Chattanooga's together.

In fact, they were just there the other night. Milton and Flora felt like eating in the car somewhere. Somewhere with a nice view.

When they pulled up to the intercom to place their order, Milton and Flora both heard Victor's voice on the intercom.

VICTOR

Hello and welcome to Chattanooga's. How may I take your order?

MILTON

Hey, Victor! How are you doing?

He immediately recognized Milton's voice.

VICTOR

¡Hey, Caballero! Bien gracias, ¿y tú?

FLORA

Hola Victor!

VICTOR

Señorita Vasconez, ¡Cómo estás!

FLORA

¡Bien gracias, Victor!

VICTOR

Excellante, mis amigos! What can I get for you lovebirds tonight?

MILTON

Uh, I'll have the nacho combo and what do you want, Flora?

FLORA

I'll have the milkshake and fries combo, Victor, por favor.

VICTOR

Alright! One nacho combo and one milkshake combo? Anything else?

MILTON

No, thanks, Victor. That's it for tonight!

VICTOR

Perfecto, Senor. That's $13.65.
I'll see you at the window.

MILTON AND FLORA

Gracias, Victor.

Milton pulled around through the drive thru lane and noticed only one car in front of us.

MILTON

Alright, the line's not too bad tonight.

Milton and Flora both looked at their phones and began to scroll through their apps, patiently waiting for their food. They were both hungry, but happily only moments away from receiving their order.

Suddenly, loud music could be heard coming closer and closer from behind them. Startled, they both turned around and noticed a loud bunch of young teenagers blasting club-house music. It was the same group of youngsters who heckled Milton exactly one year ago to this date. Milton and Flora looked at each other thinking the same thing. Flora rolled her eyes and continued to play with the apps on her phone. Milton kept his eye on them, waiting to see what crazy antics they would be up to this time.

One of the young teenagers stuck his body out of the car and began to dance. The only girl in the jeep, stuck her body out of the sun roof and also joined in the dance party.

The girl reached down with her hand and honked the jeep's horn.

HIGH SCHOOL GIRL

C'mon damnit! Hurry up! I'm starving!

Luckily, the car in front of Milton and Flora received their food and began to drive away.

MILTON

Oh, thank God.

Milton pulled his car up to the window. Milton and Flora approached the window and greeted Victor.

MILTON and FLORA

Hey, Victor!

VICTOR

Hola to my favorite couple. It's good to see your faces!

The impatient party from behind them continued to honk their horn.

HIGH SCHOOL GUY

C'mon, stop the chit chat and
get your food already!

VICTOR

Ay-yi-yi, not these jerks again.

They both gave Victor a "tell me about it" face. Victor quickly prepared our order and carefully handed it to us through the window. When Milton reached his arm out of the window, the party from behind them could see Milton's face.

The driver immediately recognized Milton.

HIGH SCHOOL GUY

Hey, it's the water boy!

The other teenagers in the car laughed and began to chant.

HIGH SCHOOL KIDS

Water boy! Water boy! Water boy! Water boy!

Victor stuck his head out of the store window.

VICTOR

Hey! You kids should learn your manners!

They rudely ignored Victor's request and threw an opened energy drink at the window, splashing all over Victor's face. It also managed to soak Milton as well.

The teens laughed and continued to chant.

HIGH SCHOOL KIDS

Water boy! Water boy! Water boy! Water boy!

Perchance, a loud engine could be heard coming from behind them. It overpowered their obnoxious chant and loud house music. The group of teenagers slowly stopped their chant and with confusion turned around. Milton, Flora, and Victor were also curious as to who arrived behind them. To all of their surprise, a large monster truck came rolling around the back of the restaurant and parked itself behind the teenager's Jeep Wrangler.

A man stuck his head out from the monster truck's window.

HANGRY MAN

Hey, what's the hold up?

Milton instantly recognized the man's face.

MILTON

Hangry man?

HANGRY MAN
Hey, Food Dash delivery guy. How you doin'?

HIGH SCHOOL GIRL
You mean water boy!

Her friends in the jeep laughed and continued their disrespectful chant.

Hangry man noticed them heckling Milton. He quickly tucked himself back inside his truck and revved his engine. Without another thought given, hangry man drove forward towards the back of their jeep. The youngsters noticed the monster truck coming their way and quickly jumped out of the car. Hangry man suddenly executed the unexpected. He drove over their jeep and crushed it like a cheap can of tuna. Milton, Flora, and Victor all watched with their eyes opened wide in disbelief.

The hangry man backed over it and then crushed it again. The teenagers held their heads in disbelief watching their car be destroyed. The house music finally stopped and the only thing they could hear was the sound of the dead horn whining inside the smashed jeep.

Hangry man placed his car in park behind the flattened car and climbed back out of the window.

HANGRY MAN

Oopps, my bad!

MILTON

Hey, thanks hangry man!" I shouted with joy.

HANGRY MAN

No problem. And thank you Food Dash guy. Turns out you were right! It was my order! Consider this my tip!

Milton gave him a thumbs up and at last, drove away with Flora as the moonlight guided them to a romantic spot to enjoy their Chattanooga's meal.

End credits.

NEW YORK FEDERAL PRISON - JAIL CELL - INT.

NEW YORK FEDERAL PRISON - JAIL CELL - INT.

Inside their jail cell, Boris and Vladimir enjoy two dishes of Philadelphia cheesesteaks and a side of French-fries.

BORIS

Hey, Vladimir, how did you get these sand-viches again?

VLADIMIR

I was introduced to a guy who could get us anything.

BORIS

Anything?

VLADIMIR

Yea, we just have to help his friend R.J. with a favor.

Boris shrugged his shoulders and continued to enjoy his hero at hand. Suddenly, the two heard their cell door slide open. The two Russians looked up and froze with their sandwiches in their hands and their hands opened wide. It was R.J. He was a large African-American inmate with tattoos and a bald head carrying two dildos in each hand.

R.J.

Hey, boys! They call me the Rim Job!

Boris and Vladimir looked at each other with fear in their eyes. R.J. slowly inched his way towards the two cellmates. The two backed up against their cell wall.

R.J.

Enjoying your cheesesteaks? Cause now you owe me that little favor. Oh yea, that's right, I'm gonna lick those little holes of your real good! How about we start a little butt cheek to butt cheek!

BORIS AND VLADIMIR
AHHHHHHH!!!!!!!

End credits continue.

The End

About the Author

J.F Moth was born in Smithtown, New York. He attended Sacred Heart University in Fairfield, Connecticut where he studied History. He then moved to Burbank, California and studied film and animation. After California, he returned to New York and studied Art and Biochemistry at Suffolk County Community College in New York. He then studied medicine at Saba University School of Medicine. He currently teaches English as a Second Language to international students from all around the world. *The Night Dasher* is one of many stories by J.F Moth. Check out his other titles at www.barnesandnoble.com. He currently lives in Greenvale, New York.